Dead Soldiers

Also by Bill Crider
in Large Print:

Red, White and Blue Murder
Galveston Gunman
Medicine Show
Ryan Rides Back
A Time for Hanging

This Large Print Book carries the
Seal of Approval of N.A.V.H.

Dead Soldiers

Bill Crider

Thorndike Press • Waterville, Maine

Published in 2004 by arrangement with Tekno Books and Ed Gorman.

Thorndike Press® Large Print Mystery.

The tree indicium is a trademark of Thorndike Press.

The text of this Large Print edition is unabridged.
Other aspects of the book may vary from the original edition.

Set in 16 pt. Plantin by Al Chase.

Printed in the United States on permanent paper.

Library of Congress Cataloging-in-Publication Data

Crider, Bill, 1941–
    Dead soldiers / Bill Crider.
        p. cm.
    ISBN 0-7862-7104-3 (lg. print : hc : alk. paper)
    1. Military miniatures — Collectors and collecting
    — Fiction.   2. College trustees — Crimes against — Fiction.
    3. College teachers — Fiction.   4. English teachers —
    Fiction.   5. Texas — Fiction.   6. Large type books.
    I. Title.
    PS3553.R497D385 2004b
    813'.54—dc22   2004059404

Dead Soldiers

As the Founder/CEO of NAVH, the only national health agency solely devoted to those who, although not totally blind, have an eye disease which could lead to serious visual impairment, I am pleased to recognize Thorndike Press* as one of the leading publishers in the large print field.

Founded in 1954 in San Francisco to prepare large print textbooks for partially seeing children, NAVH became the pioneer and standard setting agency in the preparation of large type.

Today, those publishers who meet our standards carry the prestigious "Seal of Approval" indicating high quality large print. We are delighted that Thorndike Press is one of the publishers whose titles meet these standards. We are also pleased to recognize the significant contribution Thorndike Press is making in this important and growing field.

Lorraine H. Marchi, L.H.D.
Founder/CEO
NAVH

* Thorndike Press encompasses the following imprints: Thorndike, Wheeler, Walker and Large Pr int Press.

Chapter 1

As Carl Burns hung up his phone, he wondered if he'd ever gotten good news in a call from a college dean. No matter how hard he tried, he couldn't think of a single time.

Deans never called to say that the college's business office had uncovered an unexpected windfall that would result in a ten percent pay increase for the faculty and staff.

They never called to say that the enrollment had increased by fifteen percent for the fall semester and that the administration attributed that fact directly to the fine work of the school's dedicated faculty.

They never called to say that they were going to reduce the course load for everyone in the English Department because the administration had suddenly realized that the instructors were killing themselves by grading so many student essays every semester.

And they especially never called to say, "Good morning, Dr. Burns. I'm not calling for any particular reason. I just wanted to let you know that you're doing a wonderful job as chair of your department and as a representative of Hartley Gorman College. Everyone connected with the school appreciates your hard work and dedication."

No, more often than not they called to say that some instructor hadn't posted his office hours and that they'd better be posted within the next ten minutes, or else.

Or that a student had appeared in the president's office to complain about an instructor's outrageous conduct in class.

Or that they had wonderful news: "You've been appointed to the personnel committee. It will be meeting every Thursday at three o'clock, and there are going to be some really delicate problems to deal with this year."

But this most recent call had been even worse. It had not even been from the dean but from the dean's secretary, who had said, "Dr. Partridge wants to see you in her office immediately."

No reason given. That was the ominous part. Burns tried to remember what his latest transgression might have been, but he couldn't think of a thing. His conscience was clear, or at least as clear as it ever was.

Not that a clear conscience meant anything. He was held accountable for the trespasses of all the faculty members in his department, whether he knew about the trespasses or not, and he was well aware that the sins of the faculty were numerous and grievous. Some of the faculty, in fact, probably hadn't even posted their office hours.

Burns sighed.

"Is anything wrong, Dr. Burns?" Bunni asked.

Bunni was Burns's student secretary. She had long blonde hair and blue eyes, and she was an excellent student. Burns had recently learned that her sister would be attending Hartley Gorman in the fall. Her sister, to Burns's distress, was named Sunni. He was sure there was a good reason for the name, besides the fact that it rhymed with Bunni, but he thought it better not to ask.

"Nothing's wrong," Burns said. "I have to go over to Dean Partridge's office for a minute."

"Oh," Bunni said, nodding understandingly.

Bunni had had her own problems with Dr. Partridge, or rather with some of the policies that Partridge had introduced to HGC with her ascension to the dean's office. Most of those policies had by this time been either rescinded or become honored more in the breach than in the acceptance, for which Burns was secretly grateful. Being publicly grateful was a mistake Burns didn't plan to make.

"I'll be back later," Burns said. "If any students come by, tell them that they can wait if they really need to see me."

"Yes, sir," Bunni said. Students at HGC still said that sort of thing.

As Burns walked down the shabbily-carpeted stairs of the Main Building, he tried again to think of what Partridge could want from him. He had plenty of time to think because his office was on the third floor and the ceilings were eighteen feet high. Walking down the stairs was fairly easy, however. Walking back up them was another story.

Maybe Partridge was finally going to have the elevator installed. That would be bad news indeed for Burns, whose office was in what appeared to be an unused elevator shaft that ran up the side of the building. It was the right size and shape for an elevator shaft, at any rate. But he'd hate to be moved out of his office, even if it was slightly cramped, not to mention cold in the winter and hot in the summer. It was far from perfect, but he'd gotten used to it, along with the ivy that clung to the outside walls and scratched at his windows when the wind blew, the pigeons on the wide stone window ledges, and the sparrows that nested in the ivy. He'd even gotten used to climbing the stairs.

While Burns could negotiate the stairs fairly easily, however, not everyone could. There was no way that anyone with even the mildest physical disability could get to the third-floor classrooms. There had been a couple of "nontraditional" (translation: older) students, very out-of-shape, who had been forced to spend several minutes panting on the landings before proceeding upward to the next floor. One of them had even threatened to file suit against the college, and he was incensed when Burns, in a move that did not endear him to the administration, suggested that the student might either start for class somewhat earlier or work out on the college track every day until his endurance increased.

Maybe the student *had* filed suit. Maybe that was it. Burns tried to remember his name, but failed. It was getting harder every year for him to remember student names. He had convinced himself that his failure was not a function of age. It had more to do with the fact that by now he had taught something like four thousand students at HGC. He couldn't be expected to remember *all* their names, could he?

When he got to the first floor and started to open the door, he saw that Rose, the woman who cleaned the building, had taped a note to it. The note said:

PLEASE! DO NOT!! THROW!!
ALUNIMUM CANS IN TRASH!
PLEASE USE!! RECYCLE BIN!!!!

Rose's spelling and capitalization were a little weak, but she made up for that fault with her fondness for exclamation points. No matter how many of them she used, however, she never seemed to be able to get everyone to behave in a satisfactory manner. Burns thought guiltily of the Dr Pepper can sitting on his desk. He promised himself that he'd put it in the recycle bin as soon as he got back.

That is, he would *if* he got back. For all he knew, Partridge might fire him on the spot and have him escorted off the premises by Dirty Harry, the school's security guard. Or have him dragged to the football field for summary execution. For some reason or another, Burns wasn't one of the dean's favorite people.

He was pretty sure he knew why, but while some of the things resulting from the late Tom Henderson's murder had an adverse effect on Dean Partridge, none of them had been Burns's fault.

And while he had been involved in several other harrowing episodes during his tenure at HGC, Burns liked to think he'd been instrumental in solving problems rather than in creating them. Besides, Partridge hadn't even been here when those other things had happened.

But Burns had discovered through long and difficult experience that deans didn't always look at things the same way that he did.

That was one of the things that was wrong with them.

Chapter 2

Burns walked under the tall pecan trees that surrounded Old Main (or HGC I as a former president who was fond of numbering things had called it) and entered the Administration Building (HGC II). The college's current president had asked that the buildings be referred to by their names, not their numbers, which Burns thought was a fine idea. But for some reason he couldn't get the numbers out of his head.

Bypassing the elevator, Burns walked up the stairs to Dr. Partridge's office. Melva Jeans, the dean's secretary, greeted him when he entered. Then Melva, whose blonde hair was at least half a hive high, smiled and said, "You can have a seat, Dr. Burns. Dr. Partridge will be with you in just a sec."

So that's the way it is, Burns thought. After asking for him to come immediately, the dean was going to make him wait. It was a cheap trick, but it didn't surprise Burns. Maybe Partridge held it against him because he'd been the person more or less responsible for her introduction to Boss Napier, the Pecan City chief of police.

It had all come about during the investigation of Thomas Henderson's murder, when Burns had discovered that Partridge collected toy soldiers and Lincoln Logs. He'd known at once that Partridge and Napier were kindred souls.

Not in every way, of course.

Napier was a manly man whose idea of political correctness was tithing to the National Rifle Association, whereas Partridge had introduced and tried to enforce strict rules of Politically Correct Conduct for the HGC community.

And of course there was the fact that Napier, as a representative of the law, was just the kind of person that Partridge, former member of what at one time was known as the counter-culture, had spent years distrusting.

Finally there was the fact that Napier's tastes in women ran to green-eyed redheads, like Elaine Tanner, the HGC librarian. As a matter of fact, Burns's tastes ran in precisely the same direction, which was one reason he'd been so eager to tell Napier about Partridge's collection. Partridge wasn't a redhead, nor did she have green eyes. She was attractive in her aging-hippie way, but Napier hadn't been interested, not until he heard about the soldiers. And the Lincoln Logs.

The last Burns had heard, the two of them were quite an item. His spies had spotted them at the movies one evening, and several times they had been seen eating at the Pizza Delight, one of Pecan City's fine dining establishments.

As far as Burns was concerned, it was a match made in heaven. He hoped nothing had happened to break it up. He didn't relish the idea of having Napier back in competition for Elaine. Not that Napier had a chance with her with Burns in the field, of course.

Burns sat in an uncomfortable red leather chair across from Melva's desk and looked through the stack of magazines sitting on an end table. There wasn't anything really interesting, so Burns picked up an old copy of *The Chronicle of Higher Education*. There were no articles he wanted to read, but he had to do something. He couldn't just sit there and stare at Melva's hair.

He was halfway through an article on tenure policy when Dean Gwendolyn Partridge opened the door of her office and looked out. She wore rimless glasses, and her straight brown hair had more gray in it than Burns had remembered.

"I'm sorry I kept you waiting, Dr. Burns," she said. "I was discussing a curriculum change with Dr. Miller, and I lost track of the time."

Dr. Miller was the college president, and Burns was pretty sure that he had no interest at all in curriculum changes. But he thought he might as well give Partridge the benefit of the doubt.

"I didn't mind waiting," he said, holding up *The Chronicle* as he stood. "I was reading."

"Ah," Partridge said. "You weren't looking at the job vacancies, were you?"

"No," Burns said, though he had glanced at several of the advertisements. He wasn't planning to leave HGC, though there were probably plenty of reasons for doing so. "I'm happy where I am."

"Good," Partridge said. She looked at Melva Jeans. "Hold my calls while Dr. Burns and I will be in conference."

In conference? Burns thought. *What does that mean?*

"Please come in, Dr. Burns," Partridge said, standing aside so that he could pass by her and into the office.

Other administrative offices on the HGC campus, notably the president's, were hung

17

with photos of famous people. Dean Partridge, on the other hand, preferred prints of Georgia O'Keeffe paintings. Burns had to admit they were colorful, but he would have hated having to explain to a psychiatrist what they seemed to him to resemble.

Partridge went behind her desk and told Burns to have a seat, which he did in another uncomfortable leather chair, gray instead of red.

"How are things going in the English Department this fall?" Partridge asked when Burns was seated.

Burns wasn't sure just exactly what she was asking. Did she want to know about the student who had written a paper on *The Scarlet Letter* and said that Hester Prynne wondered about Chillingworth's "whereabbots?"

Maybe, in the interests of Political Correctness, she'd like to hear about the student in Clem Nelson's class who had described Othello as "an African-American."

Or maybe, considering last spring's Thomas Henderson affair, she just wanted him to say that so far no one had been murdered.

On the other hand, it would probably be much safer simply to say, "Things are going

18

very well this semester. No problems at all so far."

So that's what Burns did.

Partridge said, "That's wonderful. And how is the new technology working out?"

Ah-ha! Burns thought. The new technology. Over the Christmas break, computers had been installed in all the faculty offices. This was a big breakthrough for a perennially cash-strapped school like HGC. Everyone now had access to the Internet and to e-mail, and there was a lot of exploration going on as people discovered the capabilities of the electronic marvels.

Burns had a suspicion that quite a few people were using their new equipment to do something other than engage in scholarly debate with faculty members from other institutions or to do research that aided in their class preparation. So maybe that was all there was to this little visit. The dean was simply checking up.

Burns began to relax. "The computers are really great. I've joined an English composition discussion list, and the two Darryls have become real computer nerds. They've put up an English Department home page that'll knock your eye out."

"I'll have to look at it some day," Partridge said, trying to sound enthusiastic, but

Burns could tell her heart wasn't in it.

That was too bad since the home page really did look good. It provided a virtual tour of the department, with photos of each instructor in his or her office. Bunni was included as well, and there was a shot of Burns standing in front of his American literature class, waxing eloquent on some abstruse topic or other, probably the dates of spring break.

"Miss Darling and Miss Nelson are learning fast, too," Burns went on. "Miss Darling didn't even want the computer in her office, but when she found that quilting page —"

Burns stopped. The not-so-tangy taste of shoe leather filled his mouth. The last thing he'd wanted to imply was that someone was using the computer for personal purposes.

Dean Partridge, however, didn't seem to have noticed the gaffe. She was looking vaguely at one of the O'Keeffe prints. Burns looked too. He thought it was supposed to be a flower, but that wasn't what it looked like to him. He wondered if he was becoming a cliched sex-obsessed English teacher like the ones that populated certain kinds of genre fiction.

He started guiltily. Maybe Partridge had brought him in here for some sort of bizarre Rorschach test.

But the dean didn't appear interested in his reactions to the print. For all the notice she was paying him, he might as well not have been in the room.

"Is something wrong, Dean Partridge?" he asked.

"What? Wrong?" She looked down at her unpainted fingernails. After a second or two she said, "Yes. You're exactly right. There's something wrong."

"Is there some problem in the English Department? Something you need to talk to me about?"

"No, that's not it. It's . . . personal."

Oh, lord, Burns thought. *It* is *about Boss Napier.*

"I hesitated to discuss this with you," Partridge said. "It's not easy for me to talk about my personal life with —"

Underlings, Burns thought.

"— faculty members. At least on school time. Maybe we should continue this discussion later."

Discussion? Burns thought. They hadn't discussed anything as far as he could tell.

He said, "I've already taught my classes and held my regular office hours today. I think it would be all right if we discussed your, um, personal life."

21

Now why did I say that? he wondered. *I don't want to discuss her personal life at all. I want to get out of here.*

But he didn't make a move to leave.

Partridge said, "All right. I hope you'll keep everything we say confidential."

"I certainly will," Burns promised. *God, Boss Napier would beat me to a pulp with a battery cable if he knew. Why didn't I just get up and go?*

"You've solved mysteries before, haven't you, Dr. Burns?"

Burns nodded, wondering where she was headed. What kind of mysteries could she have in her personal life? Maybe Boss Napier needed help on something and was too proud to ask Burns himself.

"I've helped the police out a few times," he said. *As you know very well.*

"Yes. R.M. speaks highly of you."

R.M.? So she was on a first-name basis with Boss Napier. Or a first-initial basis. Though Burns didn't like it at all when Elaine referred to Napier that way, he thought it was perfectly appropriate when Dean Partridge did. Most satisfactory, to tell the truth. Burns began to relax again.

"I'll bet he does," Burns said, not believing a word of it. "What seems to be the problem?"

"Someone has taken something that belongs to me," Partridge said.

"Stolen, you mean?"

"Yes, I suppose so. Stolen."

"Do you know who did it?" Burns asked.

"No. I have no idea."

"What was stolen?"

Partridge looked at the painting again. "Toy soldiers," she said.

Chapter 3

"Toy soldiers?" Burns said. "Why would anyone take toy soldiers?"

"Well," Partridge said, "for one thing, they're worth several thousand dollars."

Burns twisted uncomfortably in his chair. "I remember your telling me once that you got them from a man who made his own molds, but I had no idea they were so valuable."

"Those aren't the ones that were taken. The six I'm talking about are genuine collectors' items, made by Britains just before the turn of the century. Britains made the best." She paused. "Actually, the soldiers themselves aren't worth quite as much as I said, since whoever took them left the box."

Burns had no idea what she was talking about. "The box?"

"Yes. It's bright red, and it's the original box. When children were given the sets as gifts, they usually threw away the box. That's why having the box makes the soldiers so much more valuable."

Burns was having a hard time figuring out

why a box was worth so much.

"It's the same with any collectible toy," Partridge said. "Let's say you have a Rifleman gun, a toy modeled on the one used on that Chuck Connors TV show."

"I've heard of that show," Burns said. "It was a little before my time, though."

"I'm talking about a principle here, not a TV show. The Rifleman gun is going to be worth two to three times as much to a collector if it's in the original box. Did you ever collect anything?"

"Baseball cards," Burns said. "When I was a kid."

"Do you still have them?"

"I don't think so. They were in a shoebox under my bed. My mother probably tossed them out when I went to college."

"That's too bad. Some of the older cards are quite valuable. And if you had the original wrappers, well, you'd really have something. I wasn't a card collector myself, but I assume that nearly everyone threw the wrappers away as soon as the gum was unwrapped."

"We threw the gum away, too."

He remembered the sickly sweet smell of the pink gum, often coated with some powdery substance that he could never identify. The gum was rectangular, like the cards,

25

hard, and brittle as glass. Burns and his friends used to throw it on the sidewalk to see it shatter.

"The gum wouldn't be worth much, I'm afraid," Partridge said, "even if you'd kept it."

"Probably not," Burns agreed. "It wasn't worth much even as chewing gum. But let's get back to those soldiers."

"They were hollow cast lead figures. Very colorful, very nicely done, as you can imagine from their value."

"Where did you keep them?"

"They were in a cabinet in my den, along with some other things."

Burns had been in Partridge's house only once, and he was thinking that he hadn't been as observant as he should have.

"What other things?"

"Just some other collectible items. A Malibu Barbie, some *Star Wars* figures, a 3-D movie magazine, and Elvis's Christmas album. The cabinet wasn't locked. I suppose it should have been."

It was too late to worry about that now, Burns thought. He said, "But only the soldiers were taken?"

"That's right."

Burns didn't like the way things were going at all, and he certainly didn't want to ask his next question. He did it anyway.

"Have you told the . . . police?"

Dean Partridge looked over Burns's head, probably at another of the O'Keeffe prints, thinking things over, though Burns wasn't sure what there was to think about.

Finally she said, "I haven't talked to the police."

Burns had been afraid she was going to say that. She probably suspected Boss Napier of the theft. He was the logical person, if you looked at it in the right way. He liked toy soldiers, too, and maybe even a chief of police wasn't immune to temptation.

"You really should talk to the police," Burns said. "They're professionals. They know how to deal with this kind of thing."

"There's a problem," Partridge told him.

Yeah, Burns thought, *and its name is Boss Napier.*

He couldn't say that, however, so he asked, "What's the problem?"

"The problem is the circumstances. The soldiers were stolen during a party at my house."

Burns's feelings were hurt. He hadn't been invited to any party at the dean's house.

"What party?"

"Last weekend. The party for our honor students. I invited them to my house to meet the members of our board and receive their congratulations."

"Oh," Burns said. "That party."

At a recent faculty meeting, Partridge had announced her intention of honoring HGC's top students. The football players got letter jackets, she had said, so why not do something for the scholars? A tea at the dean's house. It wasn't a letter jacket, but it was something.

"You can see the problem," Partridge said. "If word gets out that something was taken from my house, the students will get the blame. That would result in some very unfavorable publicity."

Everyone in the administration at HGC seemed concerned about bad publicity, not that Burns blamed them. There had been an unseemly number of problems at the school recently, and while everything had worked out for the best in the end, there had been some touchy moments.

"You don't think a student is guilty?" Burns asked.

"That's always possible. But I'd rather not think so. For that matter, I'd rather not think that anyone is guilty."

"Someone has to be, if the soldiers are missing."

Partridge nodded. "That's why I wanted

to talk to you. I was hoping that you could look into things. I know that you can be discreet."

Burns was getting the picture now, but he decided to make sure. "I don't know that I can do anything, but what if I do find out who took the soldiers? What then?"

"I thought you might be able to persuade him or her to return them. I wouldn't press charges. I just want to get the pieces back as quietly as possible."

Burns didn't want to look into anything or try to persuade anyone. But he couldn't come up with any good reason to refuse. He tried hard to think of one.

Seeing his hesitation, Partridge said, "It wouldn't have to interfere with your teaching or your other duties on campus. It would be very low-key."

Burns knew that he was going to be sorry, but he said, "All right. I'll do it. Do you have a list of the people who attended the party?"

"Melva has printed one out for you. She'll give it to you when you leave."

"How many names are on it?" Burns asked, a little depressed that Partridge had been so sure of him.

Partridge didn't meet his eyes. "About one hundred."

"One hundred?" Burns said. "You're kidding."

"I'm afraid not."

"But that's impossible. I can't go around questioning a hundred people. It would take forever."

"I might be able to help you narrow it down some," Partridge said.

She punched a button on her intercom and asked Melva to bring in the list. Melva opened the door, walked past Burns, and laid the list on Partridge's desk.

"Thank you, Melva," Partridge said, and Melva departed without a word. Burns thought that she probably hadn't been invited to the party, either.

Partridge looked over the list and said, "I was wrong. There are only eighty-six names here."

"That's close enough to a hundred for me," Burns said. "Could I have a look at it?"

Partridge handed the list across the desk. Burns struggled with the chair and finally managed to rise to a half-standing position and reach for the list. As he fell back into the chair, he scanned the list rapidly. The ninth name belonged to Boss Napier, and Burns felt the beginnings of indigestion. Things were even worse than he had feared. Even

Napier was a suspect.

"How are you going to narrow things down?" Burns asked.

"Many of the guests never went into the house," Partridge said. "It was a yard party."

Burns was skeptical. "A yard party?"

"Yes. I rented a tent. It was quite nice."

"What about Billy?"

"He wasn't a problem," Partridge said.

Burns found that hard to believe. Billy was Partridge's pet goat, or as she preferred to call him, her animal companion. He lived in a little shed in the yard, though Burns had never seen him inside it. Most of the time, he was standing on top of it.

Billy wasn't exactly friendly, as Burns had good reason to know, and there was no fence around the shed, either. As far as Burns was concerned, any guests in the yard were taking their lives in their hands.

"I rented a little fence," Partridge said. "I didn't know you could do that, but you can. Billy was quite happy to watch the goings-on."

Burns didn't believe Billy was happy, and he didn't believe the part about the "little fence." Billy would never have been deterred by a little fence. Not that it made any difference. What Burns wanted to know was

31

how many people could be marked off the list. He handed it to Partridge and asked her to see what she could do.

"I'll give you a call when I'm finished," she said.

Burns hoped that would be a long time, but he saw the list again much sooner than he had expected. It was the very next day.

Right after Burns found out about the murder.

Chapter 4

Boss Napier was waiting when Burns came back to his office after his American literature class the next day.

"Nice cozy little place you got here, Burns," Napier said when Burns came through the door. "Got you a computer, a view, even some birds on the window ledge."

Burns looked out the windows. Pigeons whirred and cooed and stalked around the ledges. There was something else there too, a coating that resulted from the presence of the birds. What the place needed was a good rainstorm, Burns thought, but that wouldn't help the ceiling, which was darkly stained from generations of pigeon droppings in the attic.

Napier didn't seem concerned with the stain just over his head. He was sitting in Burns's chair, his feet propped up on the desk. The feet were enclosed in low-heeled black cowboy boots that went with the western-cut gray suit Napier was wearing. The police chief even had on a ten-gallon hat.

"Don't tell me," Burns said. "Hollywood has called. You're going to be the new John Wayne."

Napier swung his feet off the desk and set them on the floor. Then he leaned forward and rested his forearms on the desk.

"You always did think you were funny, Burns," he said. "But you were wrong."

"Probably. Mind if I sit down?"

"Why not? It's your office."

Bunni was in class, so Burns took her chair at the computer desk. He put his American lit text and grade book on the mouse pad beside the computer and looked at Napier.

"I don't suppose this is a social call," he said.

"Can't put anything past you college guys, can I?" Napier said. He looked at the literature book. "Who've you been talking about today?"

"Edgar Allan Poe."

" 'The House of Usher'? That kind of stuff?"

Burns nodded, admitting that he'd been talking about that kind of stuff.

"I read that one once," Napier said. "But I didn't get it. I mean, here's this guy who goes to visit an old pal that he knew when they were kids, but he never even knew the old pal had a twin sister. I'll bet you knew if your pals had twin sisters, didn't you, Burns?"

"I don't think any of them did," Burns said.

"Well, if they did, you'd have known it. How big was this House of Usher, anyhow?"

Burns had never given that aspect of the house much thought. "I don't really know."

"It would have to be pretty big, right? It had that basement or whatever. Dungeon, maybe. Lots of rooms in a house like that, probably."

"I'm sure you're right."

"Take a lot of people to run a place that size. As I remember the story, there's some old servant that lets the guy in when he gets there."

Burns acknowledged that there was a servant.

"So what happened to him?" Napier asked. "He's never heard from again, right? Did he just take off for the tall and uncut? And what about the other servants? Big old house like that, out in the middle of nowhere, that Usher guy couldn't take care of the place, not in his condition. Somebody had to cook and clean and all that. What was his condition, exactly?"

Burns had to admit that he didn't know what Usher's condition was, not exactly.

Napier didn't care. "So anyway the old pal buries his twin sister alive, she breaks out of the coffin, gets out of the basement, and comes after him. Then the whole house falls down. Right?"

"Right."

"Well, what about the servants? The guy who rode up is the only one who gets away, so what about the servants? Did they just stay in there and let the house fall down around them? Or did they slide out the back door before the big crash? It looks to me like if Poe was any kind of a writer, he'd tell you stuff like that."

"Well," Burns said, "what happens to the servants isn't really the point of the story. You see —"

"No," Napier said. "I don't see. It's the details that matter, Burns, and Poe was weak on the details. What's that other story, the one about the letter?"

" 'The Purloined Letter,' " Burns said.

"Yeah, that one. Guy goes into a dimly lighted room. He's wearing sunglasses so dark the other guy there can't see his eyes, but he still manages to read the address on a letter from all the way across the room. You think anyone could really do that?"

"Probably not, but —"

"Don't give me any *buts*. It's the details, Burns, the details. Like that story about the ape."

" 'The Murders in the Rue Morgue.' "

"Right again, Burns. You were probably a real whiz in grad school. Anyway, in that one the ape kills the women and then goes out the window. And we're supposed to believe that he closes the window so that it locks behind him. Do you believe an ape would do that, Burns?"

Burns said that he wasn't sure.

"Me neither," Napier said. "But if I were betting, I'd bet against the ape. Apes in general aren't that polite. That window's another detail, Burns, but an important one."

"I always enjoy discussing literature with you," Burns told him, "but somehow I don't really think you came here to give me your views on the short fiction of Edgar Allan Poe."

"Right again. You're sharp as an icepick today, Burns."

Burns didn't feel particularly sharp. What he felt was worried. When Boss Napier dropped by your office, it wasn't a good sign. Visits from Boss Napier, in fact, ranked right up there with telephone calls from deans.

"Why did you come, then?" Burns asked.

"I told you," Napier said. "Details."

"Such as?"

"Such as Matthew Hart. You ever hear of him?"

"Of course I've heard of him. He used to teach here at HGC, but he found a way to make a lot more money. Now he sells insurance."

"Sold, Burns. He *sold* insurance."

"He's retired?"

"No, Burns. I got you that time. He hasn't retired. He's dead."

"I'm sorry to hear it," Burns said. "I'll bet he was well-insured."

"Very funny, Burns. I'm sure his family will get a big laugh out of that one."

Burns was nonplussed. Boss Napier — Mister Sensitivity? That was about as likely as Woody Allen winning an Arnold Schwarzenegger look-alike contest. Something was really off-kilter.

"I didn't mean to be callous," Burns said. "I'm just trying to figure out what's going on here."

"What's going on is that Matthew Hart is dead," Napier said.

Burns was getting uneasy. "He was getting up in years. It happens."

"Not the way it happened to Hart."

Uh-oh, Burns thought. *Here it comes.*

"How did it happen?" he asked, not really wanting to hear the answer.

"Somebody shot him, that's how."

"Was it an accident?" Burns asked, hoping that Napier would say *yes.* "Who shot him?"

"I don't know who shot him," Napier said. "Not yet, anyway. And it wasn't an accident. It was murder."

Burns felt his stomach go hollow. It wasn't just the murder; it was the fact that Napier was telling him about it. Napier would never do that if he didn't think that Burns were somehow connected to the crime.

"What does it have to do with me?" he asked.

"What have I been telling you, Burns? Details. It's all in the details."

"I don't know what details you're talking about."

"Maybe you do, and maybe you don't."

"What's that supposed to mean?" Burns asked.

Napier leaned back in the desk chair and crossed his hands over his belt buckle. It was silver and shiny and about the size of a full-grown armadillo. In fact, it was shaped like an armadillo, with little beady silver eyes.

"It just means that every single time somebody in this town dies under suspicious circumstances, your name comes into it, one way or the other. I'm getting real tired of that, Burns."

"Not as tired as I am," Burns said.

"Well, I guess we'll see about that, won't we?"

"Maybe. But right now, let's assume that I don't know about those details you keep talking about. Why don't you enlighten me?"

"*Enlighten*. Now there's a word you don't hear very often. You English teachers really do have fine vocabularies."

Burns sighed. "Just give me the details, all right? You can leave off the sarcasm."

"Sorry about that. I tend to get touchy when somebody gets murdered."

"I don't blame you. But if you're going to tell me anything else, go ahead and do it before a student comes by for a conference."

"You have a lot of conferences, do you?"

The truth was that Burns had hardly any conferences. He encouraged students to come by his office any time they needed help, but no one ever seemed to come. Not until about a day before final exams. Then one or two would come by wanting to know what they had to make on the final in order to make an A in the class. Considering that the averages of the people who generally asked that question were usually D's or lower, Burns would just as soon that they'd never come by at all.

"I don't really have many conferences," he said. "But I do have a student secretary. She'll be here soon."

"Okay, then," Napier said. "I'll tell you the details. There's just one of them really."

"Just one?"

"Yeah, but it's a good one."

"What is it, then?"

Napier stood up and stretched. He seemed to Burns to have lost a bit of weight, but Burns thought that this probably wasn't the time to mention it.

Napier looked at Burns and smiled. It wasn't a pretty sight.

"You're gonna love this detail," he said. "I guarantee it."

"I'm sure I will, but I can't love it unless you tell me what it is."

Napier stopped smiling. He stuck his hands in the pockets of his suit and stared out the window. Then he turned back to Burns as if hoping to catch him looking guilty.

"It's a toy soldier," he said.

Chapter 5

Burns didn't just look guilty. He practically jumped out of Bunni's chair.

"Got you that time, Burns," Napier said with satisfaction. "Now why is it that the mention of a little toy soldier has you so shook up?"

"I, ummm, I, well, . . ." Burns's voice trailed off. He couldn't think of anything to say. Lying had never come easily to him.

Napier brushed back his coat and stuck his thumbs in his belt, revealing a very large revolver in a leather holster. Burns would just as soon not have seen the revolver.

"It's pretty depressing, isn't it?" Napier said. "One of the college's former teachers is killed. Lying on the driveway beside his body is a toy soldier that's also connected to the school. You do know what I'm talking about, don't you?"

Burns didn't want to give anything more away, so he said, "I'm not sure."

Napier snorted. "Sure you're sure. You know where that soldier came from as well as I do."

Either Boss Napier had already talked to Gwendolyn Partridge, or he was a better observer than Burns was. Or both. Of course, he'd been in Partridge's den a lot more often than Burns had, so he would have had more opportunities to notice the toys in the cabinet.

"Let's say that I *might* know where the soldier came from. What does it have to do with me?"

Napier walked around the desk and loomed over Burns. "Why do you always have to make things so hard? You know what it has to do with you. When Gwen found out the soldiers were missing, she went right to you."

So Napier had talked to Partridge. Naturally he would have when he found the soldier. He would have recognized it at once. And he would have talked to Partridge, who would have told him that she and Burns had discussed the missing soldiers. Suddenly Napier's behavior made sense to Burns.

He said, "You're jealous, aren't you?"

Napier laughed. "Me? Jealous? You must be kidding. I don't know the meaning of the word. But when a crime is committed, people are supposed to go to the police, not an English teacher."

"Sounds like a bumper sticker back in the

sixties," Burns said. "Something like, 'If you don't like the police, next time you're robbed, call a hippie'?"

"I'm too young to remember the sixties," Napier said. "But it's a funny bumper sticker. And calling a hippie would be about as effective as calling an English teacher. All you English teachers would like to be hippies, wouldn't you?"

Burns was getting tired of Napier's act. Also, he didn't like being loomed over. So he scooted the chair backward and stood up.

"I was too young to be a hippie," he said. "Besides, I've helped you out a time or two, don't forget."

That was understating the case, in Burns's opinion. He'd done more than help Napier out. He'd solved cases for him. And the last one had been a big one, even though Napier didn't appear to be properly grateful.

"Well, I don't want any help from you this time. I've already talked to Gwen, and I know she asked you to talk to the people who came to her party, but I want you to stay out of it. This isn't just some little theft we're talking about. It's murder."

Burns walked behind his desk. He felt more secure now that there was heavy furniture between him and Napier.

44

"I'll be more than happy to stay out of it," he said. "I never wanted to get involved in the first place. Dean Partridge was going to give me a list of the people who were at her party, but I haven't gotten it yet."

Napier pulled a folded paper from inside his coat and held it up for Burns to see. "And you won't be getting it," he said. "I have it now, and I'll do the questioning."

"Good. I'll just spend my time talking to my students about Edgar Allan Poe."

"Good. Don't forget to tell 'em about the details."

Napier stuck the paper back inside his jacket and turned to go.

"Have you lost weight?" Burns asked.

Napier turned back into the room. "You noticed?"

"I noticed. Are you on a diet?"

"Yeah. I decided that I needed to drop a few pounds. Not to impress anybody or anything like that, you understand."

"Of course. What kind of diet regimen are you on?"

"Regimen? That's another good English teacher word, Burns. How many times do you hear anybody say *regimen?* Anyway, I'm not on any regimen. I just eat those low-fat frozen dinners. Budget Gourmet. Ever see those?"

Burns had seen them, but he'd never eaten one. He wasn't sure that he would ever want to. In his experience, all frozen dinners tended to taste more like the cartons they were packed in than any recognizable food.

"I pick 'em up when they're on sale," Napier said. "Under two bucks a pop. Can't beat a deal like that."

"And you like them?"

"They're okay. I don't eat snacks, either. Except for fruit. I eat an apple now and then, or maybe some dried apricots."

"Is it hard to stick to a diet like that?" Burns asked.

"Nah. And I cheat a little, sometimes. I found out that a Ding Dong doesn't have but a hundred and eighty-five calories, so I have one of those every now and then." Napier paused. "You're not trying to softsoap me, are you, Burns?"

"Me?" Burns said. "Perish the thought."

"Yeah, I'll bet. Well, it won't work. If I catch you meddling around in this murder case, I'm going to take you out to a quiet little spot that I know about and work you over with my bullwhip."

Burns had heard the stories about Napier and his bullwhip, but he'd never been quite sure he believed them. He still wasn't sure.

He hoped the stories were just rumors, started by people who'd seen too many Lash LaRue movies on Saturday TV during their childhoods. Or maybe they were rumors started by Napier himself for the purpose of intimidation. Burns had to admit that they were pretty intimidating, all right.

"You don't have to worry about me," Burns assured Napier. "I don't want to have anything to do with this. I've got problems of my own."

"You sure do," Napier said. "You're playing in a ball game on Saturday, aren't you?"

Burns said that he was.

"I thought so. I'll probably see you there."

"Great," Burns said with as much enthusiasm as he could muster, which wasn't a lot.

Murder was bad enough, certainly, but Burns had never known Matthew Hart very well. Hart had left teaching before Burns had ever come to HGC.

The ball game was different. Burns was going to have to play second base.

That made it personal.

Chapter 6

The news about Matthew Hart was all over campus by the time Burns got to the boiler room, the only place left to sneak a cigarette since Dean Partridge had been instrumental in declaring HGC a "nonsmoking campus."

"You're late," Mal Tomlin said, exhaling a thin stream of smoke.

Tomlin, the chair of HGC's Education Department, had sandy hair and a freckled face. He looked a little like Huck Finn might if he'd gone into academia.

"I was talking to Boss Napier," Burns said. "Give me a cigarette."

"You quit, remember?" Earl Fox said.

Fox was the clean-cut chair of the History Department, Tom Sawyer to Tomlin's Huck. If Fox hadn't insisted on buying all his clothes at garage sales, he might have passed as an Ivy-leaguer. As it was, he looked like an Ivy-leaguer who'd been dressed by a wino.

"That's right," Burns said. "I quit. Now I'm starting again. What are we smoking today?"

"Harley-Davidsons," Tomlin said, getting the pack out of his pocket and extending it to Burns.

Burns took the pack and looked at the Harley-Davidson logo. He wasn't sure just what motorcycles had to do with cigarettes, but there must have been a connection.

"We don't have to get tattoos to smoke these, do we?" he asked.

"Not if you don't want one," Tomlin said. "Need a light?"

"Of course he needs a light," Fox said. "A guy who doesn't smoke wouldn't be carrying around a lighter, would he?"

"Guess not," Tomlin said, lighting Burns's cigarette with a red plastic butane lighter.

Burns inhaled and felt the harsh burn of the tobacco, the tar, the nicotine, and God only knew what else. Maybe motorcycle oil. He remembered then why he had quit smoking in the first place. He took another puff. It was exactly the same, so he tossed the cigarette to the concrete floor and mashed it out with his foot.

"Son of a bitch!" Tomlin said. "Do you know how much one of those things costs these days?"

"I'll give you a quarter the next time I have one," Burns said, sitting in one of the rickety folding chairs near Fox. "Have you two heard about Matthew Hart?"

Tomlin blew a smoke ring. "That's what Napier wanted with you, huh? Professional advice from HGC's greatest sleuth."

"He didn't want advice," Burns said. "Just the opposite. What have you heard?"

"I heard Hart was shot dead." Tomlin inhaled, breathed out smoke. "Couldn't have happened to a nicer guy."

"You didn't like him?"

"Nobody liked him," Fox said, as ash drifted down onto the rayon shirt he was wearing. At least Burns thought it was rayon. It might have been nylon. Something synthetic, anyway. It had probably cost Fox all of twenty-five cents. "Did you like him?"

Burns admitted that Hart hadn't been one of his favorite people.

"The students all called him 'Hard-Hart,' " Tomlin said. "He had a reputation."

"Don't we all?" Fox asked.

"Not for being assholes," Tomlin said. "At least *I* don't. You know what I'm talking about. Hart was the kind of guy who wouldn't cut anybody any slack." He looked at Fox. "You remember that kid who was in the car wreck?"

Fox took a deep drag on his cigarette.

"The one who broke his neck?"

Tomlin nodded. "That's the one."

"Hart flunked him because he missed an exam," Fox said to Burns. "It was before you came here. The fact that the kid was flat on his back in the hospital didn't make any difference to Hart."

Burns liked for students to take tests on time, but a broken neck seemed like a legitimate excuse. Students in Burns's classes occasionally failed because of excessive absences, but the absences had never involved a broken neck. More often than not, there was no real reason for the absences. The students simply had things they'd rather do than attend class: sleep, work, or just goof off playing pool in the student center.

"Didn't the student with the broken neck appeal to the dean?" Burns asked.

But Burns already knew the answer to that one. Students appealed to the dean all the time, and for reasons much less compelling than a broken neck. Burns had even had one student in a night class complain to the dean because Burns expected him to do just as much work as the other students. The student's argument had been that he had a full-time job, and it wasn't fair for Burns to expect someone with that burden to do any reading or writing outside of class. The dean hadn't been sympathetic.

"Sure there was a complaint," Tomlin said. "The kid won, too. That just pissed Hart off."

"He's also the one who gave a class the wrong test one time," Fox said. "Or so everyone in the class claimed. He wouldn't admit it, and nearly everyone failed. I think the highest grade in that class that semester was a C."

"He was in your department," Burns said. "Did you get calls?"

Burns already knew the answer to that one, too. Everybody got calls when students made below a B. And sometimes when they made a B. These days, students always wanted A's, no matter what kind of work they did.

Fox flicked his cigarette. Ash scattered on the floor. "Yep, I got calls. I caught hell from parents for months afterward. From the students, too."

Burns was well aware that he should shut up. He'd just been warned not to meddle into the murder, after all. He also knew that Napier hadn't been kidding, or hadn't seemed to be. But Burns couldn't help himself.

"Who do you think might want to kill him?" he asked.

Fox clamped the cigarette in his teeth and squinted his eyes through the smoke that rose around his face. "You mean aside from all those parents who called me? And besides every student he ever had?"

"Not to mention the staff members who had to deal with him," Tomlin added.

"And most of the faculty members who were here then," Fox said. "And then there's me, of course. I had plenty of trouble with him."

"And just think about everybody he's screwed in his insurance business," Tomlin said. He tossed his cigarette to the floor and lit another one. "There must be plenty of those."

Burns looked around the boiler room. The boiler itself was huge. It looked a little like some kind of alien spaceship that had been trapped in a brick barn. It was wrapped in some kind of material that Burns strongly suspected had a large asbestos component.

"I wonder who found the body," he said.

"I haven't heard," Tomlin said. "You, Earl?"

Fox shook his head. "Could have been his wife. He was at home when they found him. Why do you want to know, Carl? You aren't involved in this, I hope."

"I'm not involved," Burns said.

"That's good," Tomlin said. "Because we don't want you to be distracted, do we Earl?"

"No," Earl said. "We need you at your best for the big game."

The ball game again. Burns didn't want to talk about it.

Tomlin did. "There's going to be a pretty good crowd. I think we can win, don't you?"

Burns didn't think so, not with him on the team. He didn't know how he'd ever gotten himself into this mess in the first place. It had started out innocently enough, just a suggestion that there be some sort of faculty baseball team, and Burns had never expected anything to come of it. But something had, and now he was going to be playing second base.

It could have been worse, however. The original idea had been baseball, but even Mal Tomlin, who was athletically inclined, had seen that real baseball took a lot more skill than nearly anyone on the faculty, except possibly some of the coaches and maybe Mal himself, could muster. So they had settled on softball, slow-pitch softball.

Even slow-pitch softball, however, required quite a bit of eye/hand coordination

54

and stamina, both of which Burns had in very short supply.

"You haven't looked too sharp in the workouts," Tomlin said to Burns. "I thought you said you'd played before."

"It's been a long time," Burns said.

It had been since Burns played his one season of Little League ball, in fact, but he didn't see the need of mentioning that minor point. Maybe if he'd said something earlier, it would have been all right, but now it was too late. Macho guys like ballplayers, even slow-pitch softball players, didn't back down from a challenge.

"It would be pretty embarrassing if the student team beat the faculty team," Fox said. "It might give them the idea that they're somehow superior to us."

"They *are* superior to us," Burns pointed out. "They're younger, faster, and in a lot better shape."

"Speak for yourself," Tomlin said. "Personally, I'm in great shape."

He breathed out a great cloud of white smoke and then began to cough violently. Burns, thinking Tomlin might strangle, got up and started to pound him on the back.

Tomlin began to yell and cough at the same time, not an easy trick. The yelling was incomprehensible, but Burns got the idea that Tomlin wanted him to stop hitting him. So he stopped.

"Jesus Christ," Tomlin gasped when he'd gotten his breath back. "You didn't have to do that. I was fine. Just a little tickle in my throat."

His face was red as a Martian sunset, and he was making wet wheezing noises after every third word.

"I can see that you're fine," Burns said. "You could probably go out and run five miles right now."

"I could. Faster than you could, that's for sure."

Burns didn't doubt that. Speed wasn't one of Burns's natural attributes. Even if Tomlin had to crawl, he'd be faster than Burns was.

"I don't know," Fox said. He took the cigarette out of his mouth and contemplated it. "Maybe we'd better slow down on these things until after the game."

"They are supposed to cut your wind," Tomlin admitted.

"Not to mention cause heart failure, cancer, and a few other assorted problems," Burns added.

"I can read the Surgeon General's warning," Tomlin said. "I went to graduate school, you know."

"Sorry," Burns said.

"Is Elaine coming to the game?" Fox asked, changing the subject.

"I'm afraid so," Burns said.

Humiliation was bad enough, but being humiliated in front of Elaine was going to be even worse.

"I guess she'll be cheering you on," Fox said.

"Either that, or she can give him a ride to the hospital after he pulls a hernia trying to turn a double play," Tomlin said.

Burns didn't laugh. The possibility was too real and too frightening to be funny.

Chapter 7

On his way back to his office, Burns went by for a visit with Elaine Tanner. He tried to get by to see her at least once a day, and sometimes more often than that. He entered the library through the E. R. Memorial doors, went past the check-out desk with a nod to the circulation librarian, and walked to the back of the building.

Elaine was in, but she was no longer surrounded with the many trophies that had formerly filled the room. She told Burns that she'd decided they were no longer necessary to her self-esteem.

It wasn't as if she had actually earned the trophies herself, after all. She had bought them at the same places that Earl Fox bought his clothes: garage sales. At some feel-good seminar or other, she'd heard that trophies and awards could make a person feel better about herself, no matter where the trophies came from. So she'd surrounded herself with awards for baton twirling, cake baking, good citizenship — even calf roping. The office looked a little bare without them.

But as far as Burns was concerned, Elaine was decoration enough. She had red hair, a low voice, and big round glasses that gave her a scholarly air.

"Well, well," she said. "If it isn't Jeff Kent."

Burns hadn't kept up with baseball since his card-collecting days, and that had been when he was in grade school. But he did know that Jeff Kent was the second baseman for the Houston Astros. He also knew that Jeff Bagwell was the first baseman for the same team. After that, he was pretty much at a loss.

"R.M. came by to see me this morning," Elaine went on. "He's lost a little weight, and he looks very trim."

Burns didn't like to hear that Napier had been by to see Elaine. He didn't like it that she referred to him as R.M. He didn't like it that she'd noticed Napier's weight loss.

He realized that he was being foolish, that he was feeling like a kid in junior high, that he was being possessive. He also realized that although those things were very bad, it didn't matter. He couldn't help himself.

"And what did R.M. want?" he asked.

Elaine brushed back a stray lock of red hair. "Oh, nothing much. Just to say hello.

He said something about dropping by to see you, too. Did he?"

"He certainly did," Burns said.

"I take it that he has some kind of problem."

"You take it right. Someone's been killed."

Elaine was shocked. "He didn't mention that to me. Is it someone we know?"

"Matthew Hart," Burns said. "He taught here a good many years ago, early nineties, before you came. He was in Earl's department."

"Was it an accident?"

"It was a lot worse than that."

"Oh."

"It was murder," Burns said. "But I'm not getting involved."

"I'm sure you're not. You never do."

Now even Elaine was being sarcastic. That wasn't a good sign.

"No, really," Burns said. "I mean it. Napier warned me off. It's none of my business."

"Has that ever stopped you before?"

She had a point, but Burns said, "This time will be different."

"We'll see about that, won't we?"

"We will indeed. But I didn't come by to discuss things I'm not going to get involved in. I wanted to ask you about the ball game. Are you going to be there?"

Elaine smiled, dazzling Burns's eyes. "I wouldn't miss it."

"I was afraid you'd say that."

"What?"

"I said, 'I'm glad you said that.' "

"It didn't sound that way to me."

"Well, that's what it was. I'm looking forward to getting out there and slapping the old pill around."

"The old pill?"

"That's what we pros call the ball. The old pill."

"Oh."

"It might rain," Burns said, having just thought of the possibility. "In that case, the game will be canceled."

"You sound as if that might not be a bad idea."

It wouldn't, at that. The more Burns thought about it, the better he liked it. Not only would he be spared almost certain humiliation, he might even be spared a double hernia. Or was that a single hernia on a double play? Not that it mattered. Neither alternative appealed to him in the least.

"I wouldn't want it to rain," Burns lied. "I think it's going to be a great game."

"I hope so. I hear that Dawn Melling is

going to be the pitcher for the faculty."

Dawn was one of the school's counselors, and her appearance reminded Burns of Elvira, Mistress of the Dark. Not that that was a bad thing.

"Hard to believe, isn't it?" he said.

"Because she's a woman?"

"Nope," Burns said. "We have several women on the team. Dorinda Edgely is our third baseman."

And a lot better ballplayer than I am, for that matter, he thought.

"It's just that I wouldn't want you to be engaging in sexist thinking," Elaine said. "I know you're trying to improve, but you slip up every now and then."

"I know. But at least I'm trying. You have to give me credit for that."

"You do very well most of the time. And I'll bet Dawn pitches a great game."

"I'm sure she will," Burns said. "Well, I'd better get over to the office. I might actually have a student drop by with a question."

"It was nice to see you," Elaine said, which made Burns feel slightly giddy.

He felt giddy all the way back to Old Main, and even during the stair climb, but all that changed as soon as he got back to his office. Bunni was working at the computer terminal with stern concentration, but she looked up when he entered.

"Hi, Dr. Burns," she said, reaching for a piece of paper that was lying near the mouse pad. "Dr. Partridge asked me to give you this."

"What is it?" Burns asked.

"It's a list," Bunni said. "The names of the people who were at her party."

"Oh," Burns said, feeling the bottom drop out of his stomach. "What a nice surprise."

Chapter 8

"Are you OK, Dr. Burns?" Bunni asked. "You look a little pale."

Burns took the sheet of paper from her and sat behind his desk.

"I'm fine, thanks, Bunni. It's just that I wasn't expecting to get this list today." Or ever, for that matter. "When did Dr. Partridge give it to you?"

Bunni turned back to the monitor. "Just a few minutes ago. She called and asked if you were in, and when I said that you weren't, she asked if I could come pick up something for you."

"A few minutes ago?"

That would mean that Partridge had called long after having talked to Napier, who would have told her exactly how he felt about having Burns meddle in the murder case. But she'd sent him the list anyway.

Ordinarily, Burns liked lists. He liked making them, and he liked reading them. However, the lists he liked weren't as dangerous as the one he was holding. He much preferred lists of things like "The Ten Best

Western Movies of All Time" to lists of guests at a party where toy soldiers were stolen, especially when it seemed that the soldiers were now going to be clues in a murder case.

Burns unfolded the paper and looked at the list. There were still eighty-six names on it, but some of them had been emphasized by a yellow highlighter. Burns counted them. Eleven. That wasn't so bad.

Then he noticed that one of the highlighted names was very familiar.

"Bunni," he said, "were you at Dr. Partridge's party for honor students?"

"Yes, sir," Bunni said, not looking away from the monitor. "I am one. An honor student, I mean. Anyway, I was there. I helped Dr. Partridge work on the list."

"You helped her?"

Bunni turned to face him. "Yes, sir. She talked to me about it yesterday afternoon, and we went over the names together."

"Why did she ask you to help her?"

"It was an outdoor party, and the invitations said for everyone to come around to the back of the house. But Dr. Partridge was afraid some people might forget that and come to the front door. She asked me to stay inside and answer the door and steer people through the house and out back. The names

65

that are highlighted on the list are the ones who came inside before going out back."

"So you think you saw everyone who came inside."

Bunni hesitated, then said, "I'm not sure. I guess so. But the restrooms were inside, too, of course, and somebody might have had to come in and use one of them."

Burns admitted that was a possibility. "But you saw everyone who came through the front door?"

"Maybe. I could have missed somebody."

"Did anyone hang around? I mean, did anyone stay inside rather than going on out back?"

"Practically everybody who came in hung around," Bunni said. "It was kind of hot outside, but the air-conditioning was on in the house."

Burns remembered how hot it had been. It would probably be hot again on Saturday, if it didn't rain. He hoped it would rain, and not just to relieve everyone from the heat. He pictured the softball field as a sea of mud. It was a pleasant thought, but right now, he had other things to worry about.

"So you helped Dr. Partridge highlight these names," he said, holding up the list.

"Yes, sir. It's everyone I can remember."

Burns looked at the highlighted names again.

Besides Bunni, there was George Kaspar, also known as "The Ghost." He was Bunni's boyfriend. No surprise that he was inside. Where Bunni was, there was George. There had been a little trouble between them in the spring, but that was all over now, or so Burns believed.

Since Burns was absolutely positive that neither George nor Bunni was capable of stealing toy soldiers, much less killing anyone, that left only nine names. Not that he was going to talk to them or anything, but nine would be a lot more manageable than eighty-six.

Burns sat at his desk and let Bunni get back to work. He stared at the nine names on the list: Harvey and Karen Ball, Steven Stilwell, Robert Yowell, Neal Bruce, Rex and Suzanne Cody, and Mary M. Mason.

That made eight. He'd hold off on the ninth for a little while.

Burns had met most of the eight whose names were on the list, and he knew a little about all of them. Prominent Pecan City citizens, one and all. Four of them were members of the HGC Board, the governing body that supposedly made most of the decisions about the college, though it was widely regarded as a rubber stamp for the president.

The wild card was Mary Mason. M-m-m, as her name was pronounced by nearly every male chauvinist pig in Pecan City, had made a fortune selling Merry Mary cosmetics. She drove an enormous pink Cadillac and had hair that was half-a-hive higher than Melva Jeans's. No one knew exactly how old she was, but she was single and enjoyed dating men from twenty-five to ninety. Her only requirement was that they be ambulatory. She had been married at least three times, but the marriages hadn't lasted long.

All in all, Dean Partridge's guests didn't seem to be the kind of people whose names would appear on a list of suspects in a murder case, Burns thought.

And the names weren't all that likely to be found on a list of people who might be expected to walk off with a half-dozen toy soldiers, either.

But Burns could go over the names with Partridge later, if he was actually going to do anything about them. Which he wasn't. He'd promised Napier.

Those toy soldiers bothered him, though. It wasn't so much the presence of one of them at the murder scene. What bothered him was that he'd been told about the one at the murder scene, but neither Mal nor Earl had mentioned it. That probably meant that the soldier wasn't general knowledge.

Could it be one of those little details that the police liked to hold back from the public, that little bit of knowledge shared only by the killer and the cops?

If so, why had Burns been told? Did Napier trust him that much? And if Napier trusted him, did that mean Napier, although he'd told Burns not to get involved, fully expect that Burns *would* get involved anyway?

And, to make things even more complicated, why had Dean Partridge sent Burns the list of names after talking to Napier? Was it possible he hadn't told her to keep Burns out of it? Or had he told her and been ignored?

It was all too much for Burns. He might be able to present a class with a reasonably entertaining and perspicacious interpretation of "The Waste Land," but he couldn't fathom the workings of Boss Napier's devious mind.

The police chief had sounded quite sincere, even threatening, when he'd told Burns to keep his nose out of things. But now Burns wasn't sure that he'd really meant it.

And then there was that ninth name on the list.

Burns looked at the list again, hoping that it had somehow changed.

It hadn't. It was still exactly the same, and the ninth name was still there, highlighted in bright yellow just like the other eight: R. M. Napier.

Chapter 9

Burns wanted to talk to Dean Partridge, but he had to wait until Bunni left. There was no way to have a private conversation in the office while Bunni was there, and Burns didn't want to ask her to leave while he made the phone call. He decided that he'd work on a list of his own to pass the time and to avoid thinking about either the ball game or the names Partridge had sent him.

He opened his middle desk drawer and took out a Pilot Rolling Ball Extra Fine pen and a yellow legal pad. On the first line of the pad he wrote, "The Ten Best Western Movies of All Time." Then he started writing movie names, not in any particular order but simply as they occurred to him.

The Searchers, Red River, Rio Bravo, The Man Who Shot Liberty Valence, Stagecoach, She Wore a Yellow Ribbon, Rio Grande, Fort Apache.

Wait a minute, Burns thought. *If I don't watch out, every movie on the list will have John Wayne in it.*

He thought hard and after a minute or so

wrote down *The Magnificent Seven*.

Another few seconds of thought and he came up with *Shane*.

Then he remembered Clint Eastwood. *The Outlaw Josey Wales?* Or should he put down one of the spaghetti westerns? Or *Unforgiven?* Yes, that was it. He wrote that one down and followed it with *Ride the High Country*. How many was that? He counted. Eleven. Something had to go.

He was stuck for a minute, but then he crossed out *The Man Who Shot Liberty Valence*. As soon as he did it, he heard the inkjet printer begin to crank out a page.

"I've got a test here from Ms. Nelson," Bunni said, by way of explanation. "If it's all right, I'll take it to her and then leave a little early. I need to study for a math test."

Burns told her that she could leave early and that he was sure she'd do fine on the math test. As soon as she was out the door, he grabbed the phone and called Dr. Partridge. Melva Jeans answered and put him through to the dean.

"I got the list of people who came to the party," Burns said. "I have a few questions about it."

"I'd rather not discuss it on the phone," Partridge said. "Or even on campus, for that matter."

Burns thought that she was being overly cautious, but he said that he'd be glad to meet her after school hours.

"Come by my house," she said. "I'll meet you there shortly after five o'clock."

"I'll be there," Burns said, hoping he wouldn't meet Billy again. Once had been enough.

When Partridge met Burns at the door, she didn't look happy. Burns didn't blame her. He wasn't exactly ecstatic about the situation himself.

"Come in," Partridge said. "I thought you might like to look at the scene of the crime."

"Matthew Hart was killed here?" Burns said.

"Of course not. But the soldiers were taken. I thought that a good look at the den might give you some ideas."

"I'm not so sure I want to get any ideas. I've been warned not to have anything to do with the investigation of Matthew Hart's death."

Partridge ignored his comment. "Come to the kitchen," she said.

She turned and walked away. After a second, Burns followed her. The kitchen was large and modern, with an island in the middle. Burns wondered if cooking was one of Partridge's hobbies.

"Have a seat," Partridge said, nodding toward the breakfast table. "I'll get you a drink. I have Pepsi and Mountain Dew. Which would you prefer?"

"How about ice water?" Burns said.

"Fine. I don't have any designer water, though. Will tap water do?"

"Tap water would be fine."

Burns sat at the table and waited while Partridge poured herself a Pepsi One and then fixed a glass of ice water for Burns. She brought the drinks to the table and set them on paper napkins.

"Now," she said, sitting opposite Burns, "let's talk."

"You first," Burns said.

Partridge took a sip of Pepsi. "I've already told you my story."

"Yes, but a few things have happened since you told it."

"Those things don't have anything to do with what we discussed, however."

Burns didn't want to be rude intentionally. His "You're kidding" just slipped out.

"I beg your pardon?"

"Didn't Boss Napier come by to see you today?" Burns asked.

"Yes. R.M. was in my office for a while."

"And didn't he tell you about Matthew Hart?"

"Yes, he told me."

Burns took a big swallow of ice water and set the glass back on the napkin. "Then I don't see how you can say our discussion doesn't have a connection to Hart's murder. One of your soldiers was found by his body."

"That's true," Partridge said. "But it doesn't necessarily mean anything."

Burns shook his head. "Maybe I'm just a little slow today, but it certainly means something to me. Why don't you explain why it shouldn't?"

"Let's just say that you're making a few too many assumptions. For instance, it sounds to me as if you're assuming that whoever killed Mr. Hart left the soldier at the scene."

Napier had certainly implied that, but Burns now realized that he hadn't actually said it.

"Didn't it happen that way?" Burns asked.

"I don't know, and neither do you. Neither does R.M. for that matter. All we know is that the soldier was there. What if Mr. Hart was the one who took it?"

"He wasn't at the party, was he?" Burns said.

"Of course he was. He was one of the college's major benefactors. Haven't you looked over that list I sent you?"

Burns had to admit that he hadn't looked at all of it.

"I just looked at the highlighted names," he said.

"You should have looked at the others. Mr. Hart came to the back yard, but he might have wandered into the house and taken the soldiers later on."

"If he did, then there are five more somewhere in his house," Burns said.

"Maybe. Or maybe they're in his office. Or his car. Or a safety deposit box."

"Right," Burns said, getting the point. "They could be anywhere. If he took them."

"Perhaps you could find out."

"That's another thing we need to talk about," Burns said. "Napier told me that he didn't want me to get involved in Hart's murder. He made it pretty plain."

"I'm sure he did. He has a way of speaking plainly. But remember, what we're talking about has nothing to do with the murder. You're just looking into the theft of my soldiers."

Well, that was one way to interpret things. Partridge was nothing if not devious. No wonder she was a dean. But Burns wasn't going to let her off the hook so easily.

"You didn't mention that he was at your party," he said. "Is that why you didn't want to call the police?"

"I told you about that. I didn't want to create any trouble for our students."

"And I believe you. But is it possible that you thought Boss Napier might have taken those soldiers?"

Partridge said, "Of course not," but Burns didn't think she really meant it.

"He'd seen them before, hadn't he?"

"Yes. He collects playsets, as you well know, and he was interested in my soldiers. Of course he's not a suspect."

Again, she didn't sound as if she meant it, but Burns decided to move on.

"We can eliminate the two students, too. Bunni and George would never steal anything."

"I agree," Partridge said.

This time she sounded sincere. What Burns didn't like about that was the fact that Bunni and George were apparently the only two students who'd been inside the house. If they weren't suspects, then which students was Partridge trying to protect?

"If we leave out Bunni, George, and Napier," Burns said, "that leaves us with only eight people who might have taken the soldiers."

He took the list out of his pocket, unfolded it, and laid it on the table. He smoothed it out with his hand.

"Let's start with the first name," he said.

Chapter 10

Partridge put her finger on the first name: Harvey Ball.

"We might as well include his wife," she said. "She's next, and it will be easier to talk about both of them together."

Burns wasn't sure that was true, but he was willing to go along with it.

"All right," he said. "Harvey and Karen Ball. Here's what I know about them. He's a lawyer, and his office is in the Universal Bank Building. He's on the college board, and has been for ten years. His wife took some courses at HGC a few years ago and got her teaching certificate because she wanted to get out of the house. I think she teaches math at the high school. As far as I know, they don't have any connection with Matthew Hart."

"We're not discussing Mr. Hart," Partridge reminded him. "We're discussing my soldiers."

"Sorry. I forgot." Burns picked up his glass and looked at it. "Must be something in this water."

"I'll assume that you're joking."

"Thank you. It wasn't a very good joke."

Partridge didn't smile. "No, it wasn't. Now, here's something you don't know about Mr. Ball. He's a toy soldier buff. When they go on vacation, he and his wife like to tour Civil War battlegrounds. They've been to all the major ones and a lot of the minor ones. So there's a military connection."

"Book him, Dan-O," Burns said.

Partridge just looked at him. After a second or two she said, "Another joke?"

"I'm afraid so."

Partridge frowned. "I don't think you're taking this as seriously as you should be, Dr. Burns."

She was right. But if she wanted serious, Burns could be serious.

"What's Ball's connection with Matthew Hart?" he asked.

"I told you —"

"That we weren't discussing Hart. I know that. But let's just say that I'm curious. Do you happen to know of any connection between Hart and Harvey Ball? Or Karen Ball, for that matter."

"No, I don't. You might run across something in your investigation, but I'd advise you not to do anything about it. That would be a job for the police."

Oh, brother, Burns thought. *Franklin Miller had better watch out, or Partridge would have his job as president of HGC before the year was out. She was that slippery.*

"Let's talk about my 'investigation' for just a minute," Burns said. "I'm not sure I should do anything. It might not be a good idea at all."

"And why not? You'll just be asking a few questions. Anyone has a right to do that."

"We're not talking about what rights I have or don't have. We're talking about the fact that I've been threatened with Boss Napier's bullwhip."

Partridge surprised Burns by laughing. Maybe she did have a sense of humor after all. Except that this time Burns hadn't been kidding.

"I'm sure those stories about R.M. and his bullwhip have been greatly exaggerated," Partridge said. "He's really a very sensitive person."

Sensitive wasn't the first word that would have occurred to Burns had he been asked to describe Boss Napier. It would have been much lower on the list, down around number two hundred, probably. Or lower.

"He might seem sensitive to you," Burns

said. "But you've never been threatened by him."

Partridge looked demure, or as demure as it was possible for a dean to look. "What makes you so sure?" she asked.

Now there was a line of thought Burns definitely did not want to pursue. He decided that he'd better get the conversation back on track.

"All right, forget that. Let's look at the next name. Steven Stilwell. He's an antiques dealer with what passes in Pecan City for an exclusive clientele. People come here from Dallas, Houston, and even from out of state to shop at his store."

"Yes," Partridge said. "The man's a treasure, an absolute treasure."

It figured, Burns thought. Stilwell knew how to play up to people, especially women. With his shaggy hair and rough-trimmed beard, he had a sort of slimy charm. He'd presented a number of well-attended programs on campus, and Burns had to admit that he talked well about antiques. Besides that, he'd given a great deal of money to HGC. Burns suspected ulterior motives for the gifts. Stilwell seemed like the kind of man who'd love to have a building named after him. Or maybe he was after a co-ed. He had a reputation as a womanizer.

"Antiques," Burns said. "I wonder — has he ever expressed an interest in your soldiers?"

"I don't believe that he's a suspect," Partridge said. "He would never stoop to taking something that wasn't his."

"I wouldn't be too sure of that," Burns said. "An antique dealer is a man who likes to go out in the country and find an old piece of glass that's worth a small fortune and pay someone forty cents for it."

"But that's just good business."

Yes, Burns thought, *Partridge would definitely be president of the college within the year if Miller didn't watch his back.*

"But he couldn't do business with you, could he?" Burns said.

"No," Partridge said. "He offered to buy the soldiers, but he didn't want to pay what they were worth."

"Just what did he offer?" Burns asked.

"Three hundred dollars at first. But he went up to five."

"And they're worth ten times that."

"Well, yes."

"Now, what if he had a customer for them, someone who really, really wanted them, but you refused to sell them. Do you think he might be tempted to take them if he was alone in the room with them?"

"Absolutely not. In my mind, he simply isn't a suspect. And that's all there is to it."

Burns decided not to say what was in his own mind. But he didn't agree with the dean at all. He thought Stilwell would grab the soldiers in a second if he thought there was a buck in it. And he wondered who insured all those valuable antiques. Could it have been Matthew Hart?

"We'll go on to the next name, then," Burns said. "I've known Robert Yowell for a few years now. He's a pharmacist at Pecan City Drug. I'd say pharmacists have to be pretty honest people, considering that they deal in life and death prescriptions all the time. He's also a member of the HGC Board."

"Board members can be suspects," Partridge said.

"But Yowell's not a Civil War buff or an antiques dealer, is he?"

"No, but that doesn't mean there's no connection."

Burns wondered what the connection could possibly be. He certainly couldn't think of one.

Partridge could, and she told him. "He and Matthew Hart have had several violent arguments about the college's present administration and its future."

Burns looked at his water. Most of the ice was melted now, but the outside of the glass was still beaded with moisture. Burns took a drink. The water was still cold. "I'm sure that's very interesting, but of course we aren't talking about Matthew Hart here."

"Absolutely not. I just thought I might mention their . . . rivalry. Mr. Hart was a conservative, what you might even call an ultra-conservative. He didn't like some of the recent changes on campus."

He wasn't the only one, Burns thought. Burns hadn't agreed with a lot of them himself. But the changes hadn't been all bad, and Burns, like most of the other faculty members, liked the atmosphere of academic freedom that the administration fostered. Hart probably hadn't.

"I take it that Mr. Yowell supported the changes," he said.

"Most of them. He's very progressive."

"That's good to know. What about Neal Bruce? I don't know much about him except that he works at the bank. And that he's on the board."

"His grandfather founded the Universal Bank. It was a state bank for many years, until Neal's father sold it to the holding company. Neal is still there, but he's just a figurehead. The holding company is trying to make it appear that there's still a connection to the community when there really isn't."

"And does Neal collect toy soldiers?"

"As a matter of fact, he does. He has a quite wonderful collection. His grandfather began giving him Britains for his birthday when he was just a few years old, and now he's buying Staddens for himself."

Burns took it that Stadden was another manufacturer of toy soldiers. He wondered if Napier had ever seen Bruce's collection.

"I assume that Bruce has seen and admired your Britains," Burns said.

"Yes. He even mentioned once that he'd like to buy them if I ever decided to sell."

There was something else to check on. Could Bruce have tried to work through Stilwell to get the soldiers? Or had he simply mentioned to the antique dealer that he'd like to buy them?

"What about Rex and Suzanne Cody, then?" Burns asked. "Are they collectors, too?"

"No, but they like fine things. Suzanne is on our board, and not just because her husband has made millions of dollars in the petroleum business. She's one of Mr. Stilwell's best customers, and she's given some very nice things to the college dormitories. She furnished the sitting room in the student center, too. Did you know that?"

Burns knew, of course. It was hard to miss the big mahogany-and-brass plaque just inside the door that said "The furnishings in this room were donated by Suzanne Trainor Cody, HGC Class of 1983."

"So what you're saying is that everyone we've talked about so far — except for Stilwell, Napier, and our two students — might have taken those soldiers."

"I'm afraid it looks that way."

"And you still insist that Napier and Stilwell are excluded as suspects?"

Partridge nodded vigorously. "I do. R.M. is the chief of police, after all. And Steve is, well, he's an honest man. I'm sure of it."

Burns wished he could be so sure, but he couldn't. And there was still one name on the list.

"What about Mary Mason?" Burns asked.

"Her," Partridge said. "I wouldn't put *anything* past her."

Chapter 11

After his talk with Dean Partridge, Burns drove home to change for softball practice. He put on a pair of faded jeans, a T-shirt that had a picture of a sickly green alligator on it, and some worn Brooks running shoes that were the closest thing he had to a pair of spikes.

When he arrived at the field, batting practice had already begun. Mal Tomlin was lobbing the ball over the plate, and as Burns walked onto the field, Dorinda Edgely connected and sent the ball nearly to the wire fence in left-center field. Everyone applauded, and Dorinda responded by smacking the next pitch even farther. The ball cleared the fence by a good five feet.

"Hey, Burns," Tomlin called from the mound. "It's about time you got here."

Tomlin had more or less organized the team and was its unofficial coach. Unofficial or not, he took his duties seriously.

"I had some school business to finish up," Burns said.

"Yeah, I'll bet. Well, it's your turn in the

box. Let's see what you've got today."

Burns figured that he had about as much as he had any day, which was considerably less than Dorinda Edgely. Earl Fox, who was catching, handed him a thin black bat with a taped handle, and Burns took a few practice swings. Then he stepped into the batter's box.

Hitting was not his specialty, but then neither was fielding. He didn't really have a specialty, unless you counted bench-warming. He found himself hoping that the forecast for Saturday included a one hundred percent chance of rain. Or perhaps a small tornado, one that touched down only in one spot. Say, the softball field.

As Burns tried to dig in at the plate, he looked over the field. There were no in-fielders, since batting practice was supposed to be easy. Every ball was supposed to go into the outfield, though that wasn't always the case when Burns was hitting.

Don Elliott was on the dry brown grass in right field. Elliott, who was barely over five feet tall, taught speech and drama. He was a fair fielder, and while he wasn't especially good with the bat, he figured to get a lot of walks.

Abner Swan, from the Bible Department, was in left. He usually dressed like a TV evangelist and was probably the only man in Pecan City who still owned a powder blue suit, white belt, and a pair of white shoes. He not only owned them; he wore them about once a week. Today, however, he was wearing a pair of faded overalls, and Burns, who was barely old enough to remember Al Capp, suddenly wondered if Abner had been named for a comic strip character.

Coach Thomas, who had led HGC's football team to its usual number of victories (none) the previous fall, was in center. He was in his forties, but he could still cover the territory. Not that he'd have to worry about that with Burns at the bat.

"You ready, Burns?" Tomlin asked.

"As ready as I'll ever be," Burns said, and Tomlin lobbed in the first pitch.

The ball went into a slow, lazy arch. Burns was convinced that the trick of hitting it was simple: swing at precisely the right moment of the ball's downward trajectory.

Unfortunately, he could never quite time the moment correctly, and the result was usually a weak pop-up or a slow-rolling grounder that dribbled out to the pitcher.

This time, by some amazing stroke of luck, Burns timed his swing perfectly and lofted the ball high into center field. He knew even without looking that he'd hit it farther than anything he'd ever hit before, so it came as quite a disappointment to him when Coach Thomas caught it easily, ten feet in front of the fence.

But Earl was impressed. "That was a good swing, Carl. You must've been practicing on the sly."

"Nope," Burns said. "I just got lucky."

And he proceeded to prove the truth of that statement by swatting the next five pitches feebly on the ground.

Then it was time for infield drill, something that Burns dreaded even more than the batting practice. Coach Thomas stood at the plate and hit a series of ground balls to the infielders, barking out directions just before he swung the bat.

"Get two," he yelled, knocking a sharp ground ball toward Mal Tomlin, who was playing shortstop. Tomlin was a natural. He scooped up the ball in his glove as easily as if he practiced it every day and tossed it underhand to Burns.

When things went as planned, Burns could sometimes turn the double play, and this was one of those times. He caught the ball just as his foot touched second base, turned, and threw to first in one smooth motion.

Dick Hayes was the first baseman. He

wore glasses, but they didn't seem to interfere with his ball playing. He snatched the ball out of the air effortlessly, keeping his foot on the bag.

Burns couldn't explain why it made him feel good to turn a double play like that, any more than he could explain why it made him feel good to hit the ball solidly with the bat. Throwing and hitting a ball were things that kids did, and they should have been meaningless to an adult with a Ph.D. in English from a major university.

But they weren't meaningless at all, and that was one of the reasons that Burns wanted to do well. No matter what anyone might say, there was meaning in the game itself and in performing simple tasks well.

And, of course, he was hoping to impress Elaine.

He wasn't going to impress anyone if he daydreamed, however, and when Thomas hit the next ball straight at him, Burns botched it badly. It bounced off the heel of his glove and skipped behind him into the outfield.

"And the student team scores two runs on the second baseman's error," Tomlin called out. "The crowd goes wild."

"It won't happen again," Burns said.

"God, I hope not," Tomlin said. "If it

happens in the game we're going to be humiliated."

Burns was tempted to say something like "It *is* only a game, after all." But he knew better than that. It was never only a game. There was always something else going on.

That thought reminded him for some reason of his earlier conversation with Boss Napier. There had been more going on than just the words themselves, just as there was something more going on with Dean Partridge's soldiers. There were games being played, and Burns wasn't sure of the rules.

"Pop up!" Tomlin yelled. "Your ball, Burns!"

Once again, Burns hadn't been paying attention. He looked up, but he didn't see the ball anywhere. All he saw was clear blue sky.

To protect himself he put up his glove. Then he closed his eyes and hoped for the best. The ball fell from the sky and hit the edge of his glove, then rolled over toward first base.

"We're in real trouble," Tomlin said, shaking his head. "The student team is going to murder us."

Burns wished that Tomlin had chosen some word other than *murder*. He also wished that there had been more than ten faculty members willing to play on the team. Then someone else could play second base.

But no one wanted the position. The only extra player was Walt Melling, Dawn's husband, and he was the relief pitcher. He wouldn't have been a very good second baseman, anyway, Burns thought. He was far too big and lacked the agility necessary to turn the double play.

Of course Burns also lacked the agility, too, but he *looked* more like a second baseman than Melling did.

"All right," Tomlin said. "That's it for today. We'll practice once more, on Friday. And then it's the big game. I just hope we're ready for it."

"We're ready," Dorinda Edgely said. "We'll win in a walk. Those kids won't know what hit them."

"They might do better than you think," Dick Hayes said. "They have some real athletes on their team."

"Hey, so do we," Coach Thomas said. "There's me. And there's —" He stopped and looked around at the team. "Well, there's me. But we can still do it. It just takes heart. We've got plenty of that. Don't we?"

"Damn right," Tomlin said.

"It's not the size of the dog in the fight," Thomas said as if he believed it. "It's the size of the fight in the dog."

"True," Tomlin said. "But I'd feel better about things if Burns could just hit the ball. Or catch it. Or stop a grounder with something besides his kneecap."

"He'll do fine," Earl Fox said. "Won't you, Carl?"

"Sure," Burns lied. "I'll do fine."

"OK, then," Tomlin said. "Anyone want to run a few laps, get the old wind back?"

Nobody did. The practice broke up, and Burns drove home.

Burns was hot, sweaty, and dirty. He took a shower and fixed supper, which consisted of leftover meatloaf, canned baked beans, and canned pineapple. It wasn't much, Burns thought, but it was a step above Boss Napier's Budget Gourmet. Well, okay, maybe only half a step.

While he ate, Burns thought over what Dean Partridge had said about Mary Mason. It was clear that the dean actively disliked the woman, but Burns could never quite get the reason. All that Partridge would say was that "the woman is capable of anything."

"Then why did you invite her to the party?" Burns had asked.

"Because I had to," Partridge said. "She's one of HGC's biggest boosters, and she's also a big contributor. She would have been insulted if I hadn't asked her."

"Speaking of insulted," Burns said. "Why didn't you invite any faculty?"

"I'm sorry about that," Partridge told him. "I should have, but I just couldn't accommodate the crowd. And, after all, our students see the faculty every day, and the faculty sees them. But the people of the community, even our local board members, don't have any real connection with students. I was trying to establish one."

Burns accepted that explanation. Besides, his feelings hadn't been hurt because he wasn't invited. If he had been, he probably would have complained about having to go.

So he got back to Ms. Mason. "Can you tell me some of the things you think she's capable of?"

"Anything. I'm sure she would have stolen my soldiers if she had the chance."

"Any connection between her and Matthew Hart?"

"None that I know about, but I wouldn't be surprised if there were. Not that we're talking about that, of course."

Not unless you want to, Burns thought. He asked a few more questions, but he still couldn't get to the bottom of Partridge's dislike for Mason. After a while he dropped the subject.

"So what are you going to do next?" Partridge asked.

"Go to softball practice."

"Another joke. You must have your classes rolling in the aisles, Dr. Burns."

"I wouldn't go so far as to say that. Besides, I'm not joking. I'm playing in the faculty-student game on Saturday."

"Well, well. I never thought of you as the athletic type."

"I have hidden depths."

Partridge gave him an appraising look. "You surely do. Now, tell me your plan for investigating the theft of my soldiers."

What Burns wanted to tell her was that he planned to go to practice, then go home and grade some papers. And after that, go to bed. He didn't want to do anything about the soldiers, and he most certainly didn't want to get involved in Boss Napier's murder case.

What he said was, "I suppose I could talk to some of the people on your list, maybe tell them that the soldiers are missing and ask if they saw anything unusual or suspicious."

"That might be a good way to start," Partridge said.

But so far Burns hadn't started. For one thing, he was sure that Napier, who had a copy of Partridge's list, would be questioning some of the people on it, and Burns didn't want to follow along behind him. Napier wouldn't like it, and neither would the people he'd been talking to.

Burns cleaned up the table, put the dishes in the dishwasher, and checked out the TV schedule. There was nothing on he wanted to see, which wasn't unusual, so he began rereading Ross Thomas's *Yellow Dog Contract*.

Burns sometimes felt guilty that he found reading and rereading mysteries much more relaxing than reading the kind of material he dealt with every day. But while Hemingway and Faulkner might have been the perfect comfort reading for some people, they just didn't work for Burns.

He put the book down about ten-thirty and got ready for bed. He was almost asleep when the telephone rang. He picked it up and said, "Hello."

"Burns! Is that you, Burns?"

"Yes, Mal. It's me. Who were you expecting? Jeff Kent?"

"This is no time for jokes, Burns," Tomlin said. "You gotta get over to my house quick! Some son-of-a-bitch just tried to kill me!"

Chapter 12

Burns threw on some clothes and drove over to Tomlin's place as quickly as he could. When he arrived, every light in the house was on. He checked for police cars, but he didn't see any. He parked at the curb and got out.

Going up the sidewalk to the front door, Burns looked around the neighborhood. Everything was quiet except for a couple of crickets cricketing off in the grass, and all the other houses were dark. It was just after eleven o'clock. People in Pecan City went to bed early.

Burns rang the doorbell, and after a few seconds the door opened a crack. An eyeball looked out at him.

"That you, Burns?"

"It's me, Mal. What's going on?"

"I told you what's going on. Somebody tried to kill me." Tomlin opened the door. "Come on in, quick."

Burns stepped lively, and Tomlin shut the door behind him. Then he threw the deadbolt and put on the chain. He was wearing a pair of shorts and an HGC T-shirt, and his hair was sticking out as if he'd run his hands through it several times and hadn't smoothed it back down.

"Come on back to the kitchen," he said. "Joynell put some coffee on."

Burns followed Tomlin to the back of the house. Joynell was sitting at the Formica-topped table drinking coffee from an insulated plastic cup.

"Hi, Carl," she said.

She had on a bulky yellow terrycloth robe that covered her ample body like a tent. Her usually stiffly-sprayed blonde hair was mashed flat on one side.

"Would you like some coffee?" she asked.

The coffee smelled good, but Burns wasn't much of a coffee drinker, so he declined. Tomlin poured a cup for himself and sat at the table opposite his wife.

"Sit down, Burns," he said. "I want to hear what you think about this."

Burns sat at the table. "I think you should call the police."

"That's what I told him," Joynell said. "But he never listens to me."

"He should," Burns said, thinking about his earlier conversation with Boss Napier. "If someone tries to kill you, you call the police. You don't call an English teacher."

"I don't like the police," Tomlin said.

101

"That Boss Napier has it in for me. Every time someone gets killed around here, he arrests me."

"That's not true," Burns said. "You've never even been a suspect." He thought it over and realized that he was wrong. "Well, hardly ever."

"Once is enough," Tomlin said. "Besides, it's you who solves all the cops' cases for them."

Oh, boy, Burns thought. *Boss Napier would really like to hear that.*

"We can call the police in a minute, I suppose," he said. "Now, tell me what happened."

"I told him not to go outside," Joynell said. "But he wouldn't listen."

Burns was beginning to see a pattern in her remarks, but he knew there was a good reason for it. Mal wasn't the type to listen to anybody.

"Here's the deal," Mal said. "I went outside to take Melinda for a walk, and that's when it happened."

Melinda was the Tomlins's dog. She was one of the largest basset hounds that Burns had ever seen, and her favorite pastime was eating. When Tomlin and Joynell left the house they had to jam a chair under the handle of the refrigerator door to brace it shut, or Melinda would help herself to whatever was inside.

Melinda had long ago discovered that the refrigerator was a good source of food (a particular favorite of hers was butter), and shortly after that she had figured out how to get the door open. Tomlin told Burns that he had come home one hot afternoon to find Melinda lounging on the floor, cool and comfortable in the flow of air from the open refrigerator door, with the remains of a chuck roast resting between her front paws and a nearly empty butter tub off to the side.

"I can see that Melinda might need a little exercise," Burns said.

"Right," Tomlin agreed. "So I take her out every night after the news on Channel 8. We always walk up the street a couple of blocks, then circle the old hospital and come back home."

The old hospital was a ruin that should have been razed long ago in Burns's opinion. The mortar between the bricks was loose and crumbly, and the basement was full of water that half the third floor had already fallen into.

"Melinda likes to visit the hospital," Tomlin went on. "We usually make a stop on the grounds for her to water the steps, and that's where he took a shot at me."

"Someone tried to shoot you?" Burns said.

"That's what I told you on the phone," Tomlin said.

Technically speaking, Burns thought, *Mal hadn't said that anyone had tried to shoot him.* He'd just said that someone tried to kill him. But it wasn't a point worth arguing about.

"Did you get a look at him?"

"Hell, no. It was dark, and I was scared. Wouldn't you be scared if someone took a shot at you?"

"Yes, I would. Did you hear the shot?"

"Sure. It was kind of a snapping sound. And it took a hunk out of the bricks in the wall."

"I told him to call the police," Joynell put in. "But he never listens."

"What could the cops do?" Mal asked. "Whoever shot at me would've been long gone by the time they got there."

"He took just one shot?" Burns asked.

"Yeah. You know how there's a doorway under those old stairs out in front of the hospital?"

"I don't go there often," Burns said.

"Well, you can take my word for it. There's a doorway there. I ducked back under the stairs and dragged Melinda with me. And if you think that was easy, you're wrong."

"I can imagine."

"Yeah. Like dragging a hippo. Anyway, I got back under there and hunkered down, but there weren't any more shots. After a little while, I came out and came on back home."

"I thought he'd been hit by a car or something," Joynell said. "He never stays gone for long, but this time he was gone for nearly an hour."

"OK, so I hunkered down for more than a little while. Anyway, I'm all right."

"How about Melinda?" Burns asked.

"She's fine. She didn't like the dragging part, but aside from that she didn't even know anything had happened. She's snoring away in the utility room right now."

"You're sure somebody shot at you? It wasn't just some truck backfiring?"

"I told you the bullet took a hunk out of the wall, right? Look here." Tomlin pointed to his right cheek. "See those little scratches? That's where the brick chips hit me."

Burns tried to think of some reason why a brick might explode by accident. He couldn't come up with anything.

"I'm going to call Boss Napier," he said.

"Aw, geez," Tomlin whined. "He'll just try to figure out some way to blame me for what happened. He'll call it a failed suicide attempt or something."

"I don't think so," Burns said. "Matthew Hart was killed yesterday, and now someone's tried to kill you. Napier takes things like that very seriously."

"All right, you can call him. But remember: I didn't want you to."

"I told him to call the police," Joynell said, "but —"

"He never listens," Burns and Tomlin said together.

"Well," Joynell said, "you don't."

Chapter 13

Burns called the police station and spoke to the dispatcher, who said that Boss Napier was indeed in the building, or he had been until a few minutes previously. Maybe he still was.

Burns asked the dispatcher to ring Napier's office and see if he was there. The dispatcher said, "Hold, please," and the line went quiet.

"What kind of guy works this late at night?" Tomlin asked.

"He might not do it every night," Burns said. "Or he might have been called in for some reason. Police don't have regular hours like English teachers. Or like English teachers are supposed to have. Anyway, I don't have his home number."

"It's probably listed," Joynell said. "Pecan City's not so big that people have unlisted numbers, not even police chiefs."

Napier's voice came on the line. It was not filled with delight.

"Burns? What the hell are you calling me for at this time of night?"

"Somebody tried to kill Mal Tomlin."

There was a long pause, and then Napier sighed. "I knew it wouldn't do any good to tell you to stay out of it. I knew that no matter what I said, you'd be right in the middle of things. I don't know why I even tried."

"I didn't plan to get involved," Burns said. "But Mal called me."

Napier sighed again. "I won't even ask why he didn't call us. I probably don't want to know."

Burns resisted the urge to say that calling an English teacher in the event of a crime seemed to be the first thought HGC employees had. He knew he should keep his mouth shut, and for once he managed to do it.

Finally Napier said, "Where are you, Burns?"

"I'm at Mal's house."

"I guess he's standing right there by you, right?"

"Right."

"Put him on, then."

Burns handed the phone to Tomlin and said, "He wants to talk to you."

Tomlin took the phone with great reluctance. He listened for a few seconds. Once he rolled his eyes toward the ceiling. Then he began telling Napier what had happened. When he was done, he answered a few questions and hung up.

"He's coming over," Mal said. "He doesn't want you to leave."

Burns had been afraid of that. He sat at the table and waited with Mal and Joynell, and they talked about the upcoming softball game. Napier arrived in only a few minutes, for which Burns was grateful. He didn't enjoy talking about the game.

Tomlin went to the door and then returned with Napier trailing along behind him. Joynell asked if Napier wanted coffee, but he turned it down.

"I guess you already know Carl," Mal said.

"We've met once or twice," Napier said. "Now tell me again about what happened."

Mal went over it one more time.

"I guess you're going to have to show me where you were when it happened," Napier said when Mal was finished. "I'm not familiar with the grounds of the old hospital. You might as well come too, Burns."

Burns would have preferred going home to bed, but at the same time he had to admit that he was interested in seeing the scene of the crime.

Mal led the way to the hospital building,

which sat in the middle of an entire block. The part of the block not occupied by the building was overgrown with trees and bushes and weeds.

The night was warm and dry, and the moon was bright. Burns could hear the crickets and the stirring of leaves in the soft night breeze and not much else.

"You'd think someone would have heard the shot and reported it," he said.

"Everybody's asleep," Tomlin said. "Besides, it was just one shot. Anybody who heard it would think it was just some harmless loud noise."

"What I think is that someone should put a fence around this place," Napier said. He was carrying a large flashlight, and he shined the light on the crumbling walls of the dilapidated building. "Some kid's going to wander into that old ruin and get hurt."

Burns agreed. "The lawsuit's going to be huge," he said.

"Here's where I was standing," Mal called out.

He had walked down a cracked sidewalk to some concrete steps that led upward to what had at one time been the front entrance to the building. The doors were gone now, and there was just a dark, gaping opening. Mal pointed out a place on the side of the steps, and Napier shined a flash-light on it. There appeared to be a chunk gouged out of the brick.

"That's where it hit," Mal said. "Right there."

"Don't stomp around," Napier said. "The bullet is going to be around here someplace. I'll send an evidence team out tomorrow morning when it gets light."

"Right there's the place I ducked into," Mal said, pointing out a dark doorway. "I might already have stepped on the bullet."

"We'll find it," Napier said. "You stayed in there how long?"

"Not long," Mal said. "Well, maybe forty or forty-five minutes."

"All right. Is there anything else you can think of about what happened? Did you hear anything else? See anything?"

"Not a thing," Mal said.

Burns looked around the neighborhood, trying to figure out where a shot could have come from. Napier appeared to be doing the same thing.

There were houses all around except for one small deserted building in the next block. Pecan City had no zoning ordinances, so there were sometimes businesses right in the middle of residential blocks. This one was on a corner. It had been a pharmacy, but the pharmacist had long since retired and moved away, leaving behind a building that no one else wanted to rent. It wasn't in quite the state of ruin that the hospital was, but it would have been easy to break into. And it had a good view of the place where Mal had been standing.

"I'm going to have a look at that place," Napier said, and started in the direction of the abandoned building.

He didn't say anything else, so Burns and Tomlin followed him. When they got to the pharmacy, Napier stopped and looked back at them.

"I'm going to look inside," he said. "I want the two of you to stay out here."

"Gotcha," Tomlin said.

Napier turned his flashlight on the ground and looked it over carefully before entering the building. There was a door hanging half off the hinges, and Napier went by without even touching it.

"The old town has really gone downhill," Tomlin said. "I can remember when half the people here bought things at that pharmacy."

"Couldn't compete with the chains," Burns said.

"Yeah," Tomlin agreed. "Like a lot of other places."

Over the past few years, a number of long-established Pecan City businesses had closed, unable to cut their prices to match those of the Wal-Mart and other discounters that had opened stores on the highway, away from the downtown area. There were a number of buildings downtown that looked a lot like the old pharmacy.

Burns listened hard, but he couldn't hear Napier moving around inside the building. He couldn't even hear the crickets any longer. Then a mosquito whined around his head. He slapped at it, then looked at his hand.

Missed.

Mal tapped him on the shoulder. "Look."

Burns turned and saw headlights moving slowly down the street that fronted the hospital.

"You think that's someone out for an innocent late-evening drive?" Tomlin asked.

"Probably," Burns said, though Pecan City's streets were generally deserted after ten-thirty in the evening. There were rumors that the streets were rolled up about that time, but the rumor wasn't true. The traffic lights were set to begin blinking at ten o'clock, however.

"What if it's someone who's not so innocent?" Tomlin asked.

Burns realized for the first time just how hot the evening was. The breeze that had been blowing earlier had died down to nothing, and the leaves no longer moved on the trees. The humidity had risen slightly, and Burns's face felt sticky. The car was still moving very slowly in their direction.

"What if it's the guy who shot at me, and he's coming back to see if he got me?" Tomlin asked. "You know, returning to the scene of the crime."

"I don't think people really do that," Burns said. "I think it's just an old wives' tale."

"I'll bet Boss Napier knows whether it's true or not. Let's go inside and ask him."

"He told us to stay out here. I don't think we should go in."

"I'm not scared of him," Tomlin said.

Burns smiled. "But you're scared of that car?"

"Damn right. Or whoever's in it. I'm the one who got shot at, remember? If he tried once, he might try again."

The car was going even slower now. In fact, the closer it got to them, the slower it went.

"It's going to stop," Tomlin said. "You can stay out here if you want to. I'm going in."

The car came to a stop at the curb about twenty-five yards away, and the lights went off. Burns was beginning to think that Tomlin had the right idea. Then the car door opened. The interior light came on, but Burns couldn't see the driver's face.

"Come on," Tomlin said, tugging at Burns's elbow.

Burns didn't move. He was waiting to see if the driver got out.

He did, and then reached into the car. When he turned back around, he was holding a gun.

Chapter 14

As the man turned toward them, Tomlin yelled, "Hit the dirt!" and shoved Burns hard in the small of the back.

Burns staggered forward as Tomlin dived behind a nearby pittosporum bush.

The man raised the gun and fired.

It wasn't a rifle. It was a shotgun, and to Burns it sounded like a cannon. He heard a swarm of angry hornets whir over his head. There was crackling and clinking behind him as the buckshot struck the building.

Boss Napier came barreling out of the abandoned pharmacy, his .38 in his hand.

"Put the gun down," he shouted. "Put it down or I'll put *you* down."

"Is that you, Boss?" the gunman asked in a quavery voice.

Napier turned the beam of his flashlight on the man's face. "Damn right. Now put that gun down before I have to shoot you."

The man bent and laid the gun on ground. When he stood up, he raised his hands and said, "What about those other two? You gonna shoot them?"

"'They're with me. Lock your hands and put them behind your head."

The man did as he was told. "I don't see what you're gettin' so hot about. All I did was try to protect my property."

"Your property?" Napier said. "Who the hell are you?"

"Ben Dabney. That's my land you're on, Boss. I guess you could say you're trespassin'."

"What the hell," Napier said, jamming the .38 into its clamshell holster. "Come on up here, Ben."

While Dabney was walking toward them, Burns went to the pittosporum bush. Mal was still there.

"You can come out now," Burns said. "I think the guy's harmless."

"Oh, yeah? Then why did he try to kill us?"

"I don't think he was trying to kill us. He shot over our heads. He thought we were breaking into his building."

"Well, I wasn't. Napier was. Why didn't he shoot at Napier?"

"We were more convenient targets. Come on out, and let's see what's going on."

Mal crawled from beneath the bush, stood up, and brushed himself off. He didn't seem inclined to move any closer to Napier, however, so Burns went back alone.

Napier was talking to Dabney. "I want to know what the hell you were shooting at," he said.

"I just came to check on my property," Dabney said. "And I saw two men up here. One of 'em made a run at me, so I fired off a warning. Can I take my hands down now?"

"Go ahead," Napier said.

Dabney unclasped his hands and lowered them.

Burns couldn't tell how old Dabney was, exactly. In the moonlight, he looked anywhere from seventy to a hundred. His face was lined with wrinkles, and a thin fringe of hair stuck out all around the Astros cap he was wearing.

"How did you know we were here?" Burns asked him.

"Heard it from Lank Hamilton," Dabney said. "He lives right over yonder, and he heard somethin' that sounded like a rifle shot earlier. Didn't pay it much mind, but later on he saw some fellas messin' around the hospital. When you came up here to the pharmacy, he gave me a call."

"Do you own the hospital building?" Napier asked. "Or just the pharmacy?"

"Both of 'em. I didn't mean to shoot at

the law, Boss. Is this fella one of your officers?"

Napier looked at Burns. "Not hardly. Wait a minute, that's a double negative or something. He might arrest me since he's an English teacher."

"English teacher?" Dabney said.

"Never mind," Napier told him. "I'd advise you to get a fence put around that hospital building, Mr. Dabney, either that or have it torn down all the way. Somebody's going to get hurt there if you don't. And if I were you, I'd do something about this place, too."

"I been thinkin' about that," Dabney said. "I'll start workin' on it tomorrow morning, for sure."

"Wait until I call you and tell you to get started. And hire you some good help."

"All right. Can I go home now?"

"Go ahead," Napier said. "Don't forget your twelve gauge."

"I won't. Can I ask you one thing?"

"What?"

"What are y'all doin' up here, anyhow?"

"That's police business, Mr. Dabney. We didn't disturb your property, though, and it's not anything that you need to worry about."

Dabney wasn't satisfied. "I'd like to

know about it, anyhow."

"I'll let you know later on, when it's all cleared up," Napier said. "Now you just get your shotgun and go on home."

Dabney turned away and walked back toward his car. When he reached the shotgun, he picked it up and then put it in the back seat.

"I guess we showed him," Tomlin said at Burns's right shoulder.

"We sure did," Burns said. "I'll bet his knees are knocking together like castanets right about now."

"Shut up, you clowns," Napier said. "It's a wonder Dabney didn't kill you. What did he mean, saying that one of you made a run at him?"

"It might have looked that way," Burns said. "But nobody ran at him. Mal pushed me."

"Sure, blame it on me," Tomlin said. "I was just trying to save your life."

"Never mind," Napier said. "I'm sorry I asked. Tomlin, you go on home. I want to have a little talk with Burns."

Burns didn't like the sound of that. A private talk with Boss Napier was worse than a phone call from a dean.

"I'd better go on with Mal," Burns said. "I don't want him to get lost."

Mal gave them a questioning look.

"Forget about it, Burns," Napier said. "Tomlin's going home, and you're sticking around. Isn't that right, Tomlin?"

"Absolutely," Mal said. "I'm practically there already. See you later, Carl." He didn't add, "I hope," but his tone left no doubt that he meant it.

When Mal was a few yards away, Napier said, "And don't talk to anyone about this."

Mal promised he wouldn't. Napier took Burns's arm and said, "I want to show you something."

Burns hoped it wasn't a bullwhip. "I don't want to see anything. I'm staying out of this, just like you told me."

"Too late," Napier said. "I really didn't want you mixed up in this, but it's just not going to work out. It never does when you're around. You're in."

"I don't want to be in."

"Quit your whining. You're in, and that's that."

Burns didn't like it, but he didn't argue any more.

When they got to the doorway of the pharmacy, Napier said, "Stop here. We're not going inside. I wouldn't want you to touch anything and screw up the crime scene."

"Crime scene?"

"That's right." Napier directed the beam of his flashlight through the doorway and into the deserted building. "See that?"

"See what?" Burns said. The floor was littered with trash: old papers, rat-chewed boxes, an empty plastic Coke bottle or two. "I see a lot of stuff."

"That," Napier said. "Right there."

Burns saw it then. Next to one of the Coke bottles. A toy soldier. It appeared to be wearing some kind of British uniform, but Burns couldn't be sure. Maybe he should make a visit to a good optometrist.

"All right," he said. "I see it."

"I'm leaving it there for the evidence team, but I'm sure it's another one from Gwen's collection."

Burns was equally convinced. It wasn't likely that there were a whole lot of toy soldiers lying around Pecan City.

"The part about a soldier being by Hart's body wasn't in the paper," Burns said.

"That's right."

"So not just everybody knows about it."

"Right again. You're on a roll, Burns."

"You told me about it, though. Who else knows?"

"Nobody except the people on the case, Gwen, and the killer."

"It's nice to be trusted."

"Don't get too comfortable with the idea."

Burns said he wouldn't. He looked at the soldier again.

"How did it get there?" he asked.

"Think about it, Burns. I know you're not a trained crime fighter like me, but since people keep on calling you when there's trouble, you should at least make an effort."

"Somebody dropped it," Burns said.

"Not bad. Now why would anyone drop a toy soldier in a place like this?"

"He was playing war and his mama called him home?"

"Always being a smart-ass, aren't you, Burns? As police chief, I could shoot you for stuff like that. No jury in the world would convict me."

He was probably right. Burns said, "OK, let's say the guy who shot at Mal was hiding right here. He was planning to kill Mal and leave the toy soldier near the body. But when he didn't kill anybody, he panicked and left in a hurry. He didn't even notice he'd dropped the soldier."

"Not bad, Burns. Next thing I know, you'll figure out why that ape closed the window."

"I could be wrong, you know."

"Sure you could. Maybe you are. But it

makes sense to me."

Which meant he'd been thinking the same thing, Burns thought. "Do you think there are any fingerprints on it?"

"Look at it, Burns. It's too small for fingerprints. Probably too small for even a partial. It would be nice if the guy had been handling one of those plastic bottles, but I'd guess the chances of that were somewhere between slim and none."

Burns guessed the same thing. "But if he wasn't wearing gloves, he might have left prints in there somewhere."

"It's possible, but there weren't any prints at the first scene. Even if we find prints, if they aren't on file, they won't help us any until we catch the killer."

"By *we,* you mean you and the police force, right?"

"You're a card, Burns. I'll bet you crack the students up every day. You should get your own TV show."

"So you mean me and you."

"And the force."

"We need to talk."

Napier looked around them at the night and the old pharmacy building. He looked up at the cloudy sky. Then he said, "I thought that's what we were doing."

"There's talk, and then there's talk. For

one thing, I don't know about the first scene."

"Don't you read the newspaper? I thought you English teachers read all the time."

Burns had seen the account of Hart's murder. In the fashion typical of the offend-no-one policies of the Pecan City paper, it had said as little as possible, and in fact it would have been hard to determine from reading it that Hart had been murdered. It could just as well have been that he had suffered a fatal heart attack while baking an apple pie.

"I read it," Burns said. "Let's see. What were you telling me about how it's the details that matter?"

Napier slapped his neck, then looked at his hand. "Isn't it too early for mosquitoes?"

"No, but I don't believe you were really being attacked by one. You're just changing the subject."

"Okay, maybe you have more detective skills than I thought. I'll admit that the paper was a little skimpy on details."

"So are you going to fill me in?"

"Not standing here with these mosquitoes. Let's go to my house."

Burns had visited Napier's place before, but he wasn't eager to return. You never knew when the Boss might want to try out his bullwhip on you.

"You have anything to drink?" Burns asked.

"Pepsi One. Just one calorie."

"Just what I need," Burns said. "Let's go."

Chapter 15

For years Burns had driven a 1967 Plymouth. He had loved its wide bench seat in the front, with room for four passengers to sit in comfort. It was a four-door hardtop, and he had liked the look, if not the safety, of having no center post. He hadn't much liked the fourteen miles per gallon of gas that the car got, however, and so during the most recent rise in gas prices he had sold the car to someone who had been looking for one like his parents had owned when he was in high school.

"You can't believe how much room there was in that back seat for making out," the man had told Burns. "It wasn't the sportiest car around. In fact, it was pretty clunky looking. But you couldn't beat it for a date car."

Burns didn't ask about the man's no-doubt wonderful memories of what had transpired in the back seat of the well-remembered Plymouth. He just jacked up the price of his own car a little more, and in the end he had gotten more for it than he had ever hoped to receive. Then he had gone out and bought himself a Toyota Camry.

It wouldn't hold nearly as many people, but then Burns didn't plan to have eight people in the car any time soon. Besides, he could park the Camry in about one-third the space that the Plymouth had required.

There wasn't much room in the Toyota's back seat for making out, but Burns felt he was too old for making out in the back seat. He preferred a less awkward setting these days, not that he got that much opportunity to make out.

At any rate, he quite enjoyed the Camry, which got excellent gas mileage and even had a CD player, a big improvement over the Plymouth's AM radio.

The Plymouth had been dark green with a black top, while the Camry was a sort of a nondescript sandy color, but that didn't matter to Burns, who tooled along the street to Napier's house as he listened to Warren Zevon's *Excitable Boy* CD. He sang along on "Lawyers, Guns, and Money," identifying strongly with the character in the song who needed the items listed in the title because "the shit had hit the fan." That seemed to Burns to sum up his own situation admirably. He was going to miss old

Warren and his insights into life.

Boss Napier lived in a perfectly ordinary house on a perfectly ordinary street. Burns parked the Camry at the curb and went up to the porch. He looked for the doorbell, but Napier was waiting for him and opened the door before Burns had a chance to ring.

"Come on in," Napier said, and Burns did. He followed Napier into the kitchen where he saw that there was a playset on the table.

"What's that?" he asked.

Napier surveyed the small figures with a collector's pride. "It's a David and Goliath playset. Just came today, from some Christian outfit called Rainfall. Not bad, either. Twenty-four Israelites and twenty-four Philistines. That's David there, a two-incher. And that big four-inch guy is Goliath."

"Great," Burns said. What else could he say?

Besides the figures Napier had named, there were a couple of tents, some rocks, a few trees, and some animals. The trees were stunted and the animals looked silly (the sheep were as big as the single lion), but Burns supposed he'd see it differently if he were afflicted with the same mania that Napier was.

"Got 'em all for about fifteen bucks," Napier said. "I'll put them in the room where I keep the other playsets after I mess with them a little longer."

"Don't move them on my account. I think the biblical setting might be good for us. We need to talk about bearing false witness."

Napier stiffened. "Is that a crack? Because if that's a crack, I'm not going to offer you anything to drink."

"It's not a crack," Burns said. "It's just that I'm tired of being jerked around."

"Nobody's jerking you around."

"You are, and Dean Partridge is. Both of you plotted to get me involved in this mess from the beginning, but neither one of you will admit it. I'm not going to stay here one minute longer if you don't come clean."

"You want a Pepsi One?"

"I'm not drinking a thing until you tell me the truth."

"Just sit down and calm down. Then we'll talk."

Burns sat down. He didn't know what had gotten into him. Ordinarily he'd never challenge Boss Napier. Maybe it was the proximity to the David and Goliath figures. Even a David got lucky every now and then.

"I'll take a glass of water," Burns said.

"I don't have any of that fancy stuff."

Burns had a strong sense of *deja vu*. "You and Dr. Partridge are a lot alike, you know that?"

Napier looked at him through slitted eyes. "Is that another crack?"

Burns sighed. "No, it's not a crack. It's just an idle comment. How about that water?"

Napier had an industrial-sized stainless steel refrigerator that looked brand new. There was a water spigot in the door, along with an ice dispenser.

"Pretty swanky," Burns said as Napier filled a glass with water.

"The old one cratered on me, so I just went the whole hog." Napier set the water on the table. "You sure you don't want a Pepsi?"

"I'm sure," Burns said, and took a sip of his water.

Napier got a can of Pepsi One from a can dispenser inside the refrigerator. He didn't bother to get a glass. He popped the tab and drank straight from the can.

"So," Burns said. "Time for the truth-telling?"

Napier set his can on the table. He picked up one of the Israelites, or maybe it was one of the Philistines, from the playset and rolled it around between his thumb and forefinger. Then he put it back down on the table.

"Well?" Burns said.

"All right, I admit it," Napier said, looking at the figures and not at Burns. "I told Gwen to get you involved if she wanted to. She didn't want me to know she'd gone to you about the soldiers at first, but then she told me about it. And it made sense. You've been a little helpful now and then."

Burns thought it was nice of Napier to admit it, and he wished he had it on tape.

"So why make such a big show of telling me to keep my nose out of things?"

"Because I know you, and I knew that's what you'd expect me to say. I also knew it wouldn't do a damn bit of good. You just can't keep your nose out of things that don't concern you, can you, Burns? It's a constitutional weakness, and you couldn't change if you wanted to, which you don't."

"Well, I do have a tendency to get interested in things."

"Yeah. Right. And you get in trouble, too, don't you?"

Burns sat up a little straighter in his chair. "That's never been my intention."

"Don't start with the intentions. We all know about that road where they're used for paving stones."

"Okay, forget it. Let's just get down to business. Tell me how Matthew Hart was killed."

Napier took a drink of Pepsi, then said, "He was shot."

"That part, I know. You told me earlier. When, where, how? Those are the details I'm lacking."

"First let me ask you about your buddy Tomlin."

"What for?"

"Because I want to. Does he walk that dog of his every night?"

"Every night after the news," Burns said. "He told me that himself."

"And that's where he made his mistake. He fell into a routine. Potential murder victims should never fall into a routine."

"I sort of get the feeling that Mal didn't regard himself as a potential murder victim."

"Yeah. Well, a man can't be too careful."

"What's that supposed to mean?"

"It means that Matthew Hart had a routine, too. Every morning he got up at seven o'clock, right on the dot, and as soon as he'd shaved and brushed his teeth, he went out to his driveway and brought in the newspaper. Between twenty and thirty minutes after he got up. Every single day. And that's what he was doing wrong. He got shot in his driveway when he went for the paper."

"So somebody had been watching him."

"And somebody had been watching your pal Tomlin, too."

"There was a good hiding place where Mal walked the dog," Burns pointed out. "What about near Hart's house?"

"Hart lives out in the Heights," Napier said.

The Heights was an older part of Pecan City, named because it was a little higher in elevation than the rest of the town. Recently a builder had started a new addition to the area, and some of the homes had nothing across the street from them except some uncleared woods.

"Let me guess," Burns said. "Hart bought one of the new houses out there."

"That's right. Hadn't been in it for more than a month, but his routine had been the same ever since he quit teaching, according to his wife. After he read the paper, he'd get dressed and go to work. But this time somebody just hid out in the trees across the street and nailed him as he bent over to pick up the paper. Bullet went right into the top of his head."

Burns didn't like to think about what kind of mess that might have made, but Napier told him anyway.

"He was shot with a .22. If we find a slug at that old hospital, I'd bet it'll be a .22 as well. A rifle of that caliber doesn't make much noise at all, which is one of its good points if you're shooting in a residential area. You have to be a pretty good shot to kill somebody with one, but a head shot generally works. A slug that size, it just sort of bounces around inside the skull and scrambles the brain like an egg."

"Thanks for sharing that," Burns said.

Napier shrugged. "You wanted details. Now you have some."

"Right. So now I want to know how the toy soldier got there with Hart."

"Whoever shot him probably threw it across the street. It was lying about five feet from the body, a little scratched up from hitting the concrete."

"Which of course leads us to the really important question. What do the soldiers have to do with all of this?"

Napier took another swallow of Pepsi, tilting the can back to get most of what remained. He set the can on the table, and Burns looked at him quizzically.

"Well?" Burns said.

"Damned if I know," Napier told him.

Chapter 16

Napier put his Pepsi can in a recycling bin by his new refrigerator and asked if Burns wanted any more water. Burns didn't, so Napier took his glass and set it in the sink.

"Anyway," Napier said when he was seated at the table again, "the question about the soldier isn't the only important one we need to ask."

"All right," Burns said. "I'll bite. What's another one?"

"Another one is: what's the connection between Tomlin and Hart and the soldiers? Who'd want to kill them and leave a soldier with the bodies?"

Burns resisted the strong temptation to say that *among* was the proper word rather than *between*. No need to irritate Napier unnecessarily.

Burns had wondered about the connection, too, and he and Dean Partridge had talked about that point, but they had come to no conclusions.

Now that a soldier had turned up near where someone had tried to shoot Mal

Tomlin, it seemed clear to Burns that the soldiers hadn't been taken because of their intrinsic value. Whoever took them wanted to leave them near the bodies of his victims. That didn't mean that the people who had tried to buy the soldiers from Dean Partridge were off the hook, however. They were all well aware of the soldiers' existence and would have known where to find them, no matter what use they had for them.

"We live in a funny world, Burns," Napier said. "You know that?"

"I'm not laughing," Burns said.

"I didn't mean funny like that. I was talking about irony. Being an English teacher, you should know all about irony."

"I don't see any irony in people being killed."

"You just aren't looking at the big picture. If you think about some sniper killing people, you don't think about a place like Pecan City. You think about those two nutjobs up in the D.C. area."

"I see what you mean. We're supposed to be living in a safe small-town environment."

"Yeah. It's just like the Homeland Security people keep telling us. Nobody is safe anywhere, not any more."

"I don't think we're in much danger of terrorist activity around here," Burns said.

"I just can't see them targeting Pecan City."

"No, not terrorists. But there are nut-jobs everywhere."

"And you think that's what we have here? Some deranged veteran of the war with Iraq, maybe, has come home to keep on killing, leaving the toy soldiers as a clue?"

"I don't much believe in those deranged veteran stories," Napier said. "But there's a connection somewhere. Not just between Tomlin and Hart, but between both of them and the soldiers."

"Tomlin isn't a veteran of any war. What about Hart? Did you check?"

Napier gave him a disgusted look. "I know I don't sit around reading *The Sound and the Fury*, but I know how to do my job. Of course I checked. Hart never fought in a war, and he wasn't even a member of the National Guard. Didn't take R.O.T.C. in college, either."

"I don't have my list of names with me. The ones Dr. Partridge gave me, I mean. Have you checked all of them out, too?"

Napier just looked at him.

"Okay, no harm in asking. What did you learn about them?"

"Neal Bruce is the only one with military experience. He was in Vietnam, and don't give me any Rambo theories. He's a banker and wears a tie to work every day."

"Guys with ties don't kill people?"

"Sure they do. I just meant he isn't any crazed vet with homicidal tendencies."

"Neither was Rambo until somebody ticked him off."

"Spare me the psychology. You're an English teacher, remember?"

"I get the point. So where does that leave us?"

Napier stood up and stretched. "There has to be a connection between Hart and Tomlin and the killer."

There was that *between* again. Burns let it pass.

"And there has to be some connection between all of them and the soldiers," Napier continued. "We just don't know what it is. Maybe you can figure it out, sort of like you figure out what all the symbolism means when you read a poem."

"Soldiers are symbols of war," Burns said. "The only war we've had lately is the one in Iraq, where the people are now enjoying the fruits of democracy."

"I happen to be one of the people who approved of that war, Burns, so don't bring any of your wussie pinko politics into this, all right?"

Burns yawned.

"Am I boring you, Burns?" Napier said. "Because I wouldn't want to bore you."

"You're not boring me. It's late, and I'm sleepy. And I have an eight o'clock class tomorrow."

"Well, you'd better go, then. You need your sleep. You don't want to bore the students and have them yawning in your face when you're trying to explain something like why it's so important to not split an infinitive."

Burns gave him a quick look, but Napier's face showed nothing.

"You're going to have a talk with some of the people on that list tomorrow, aren't you, Burns?"

"I might, if I have time."

"Oh, I have a feeling you'll find the time. Try not to aggravate them too much."

"Aggravate? Me?"

"Yeah, you. And while you're at it, try to come up with some answers to those questions we've been talking about."

"Sort of like a take-home exam, right?"

"Call it what you want to. The sooner we find the answers, the less chance there is of someone else getting shot at or killed."

That possibility was what had been bothering Burns more than anything. He said, "You think he'll take another shot at Mal?"

"Who knows? He might, or he might go after someone else. It's like I told you: we live in a crazy world."

"You got that right," Burns said.

"Have," Napier said.

Burns looked at him.

"You *have* that right. *Got* is the wrong verb."

"I know that. It's just an expression."

"Yeah. I just wanted you to know that I knew what was right. Just in case you were wondering."

"I wasn't," Burns said.

It was after midnight when Burns got home. He brushed his teeth and got into bed, but he couldn't sleep. He kept thinking about the list of suspects and wondering how any of them could be guilty of murder. No one on the list seemed capable of that act to Burns, though he admitted to himself that he didn't know any of them very well. When he finally drifted off, he dreamed of toy soldiers and dead men with bullet holes in their heads and scrambled brains.

The next morning Burns felt terrible. He hadn't slept well at all, and the inside of his mouth tasted as if a condor had nested there. He was feeling a little better by the time he got to the college, but not by much, and the climb to the third floor of the Main Building didn't help. One of these days he was going to have to get in shape.

Usually he liked to get to school at least forty-five minutes before class, which gave him time to read the morning paper and gather his thoughts before facing his students. Today he barely had time to grab his textbook and papers and get to the classroom before everyone decided he wasn't coming at all and walked out. He made it with a few minutes to spare, and he tried to ignore the disappointed looks he saw on a couple of faces.

The course was American lit, and about half the class looked as if they were even sleepier than Burns, which wasn't unusual in an eight o'clock class. Many of them always looked sleepy.

Burns didn't take pity on them, however. He passed out the pop test that he had planned to give and waited patiently while they completed it. He took it up, gave them the answers, and started his discussion of Francis Macomber's short, happy life. A few students were actually interested in the story because of the ending. They'd had an argument before class about whether

Macomber's wife had killed him deliberately or whether it had been an accident. Burns, feeling a little like Boss Napier, told them to look for the details in the story, and then base their decision on what they found. He told them it would be fine even when they came to different conclusions, as long as there was evidence in the story to support them. This got the rest of the class, or at least the ones who'd actually read the story, interested. By the time the bell rang, Burns was feeling pretty good, almost like a real teacher.

The feeling deserted him almost as soon as he reached his office. Bunni was at the computer, and she told him that he'd had a call from the dean.

Deja vu all over again, he thought, knowing that the dean herself hadn't actually done the calling. That would have been a job for Melva Jeans.

"Does she want me to return the call?" he asked.

"Yes," Bunni said. "She said it was important."

That was another thing about calls from deans, Burns thought. They were always important, and they always had to be returned. Okay, that was two things. But the point was the same in any case. He reached for the phone, but it rang before he could pick it up and make his call.

"This is Carl Burns," he said. "How may I help you?"

He answered that way only because there had been a called faculty meeting about telephone etiquette. It had somehow come to the president's attention that the campus phones were not being answered in a courteous fashion, either by the student workers or the faculty. Why, some people were actually just saying *hello* instead of informing the caller of who was speaking.

Burns had always figured that the caller should know who was speaking, having placed the call to that person's office, but he didn't express that thought to the president. Instead he sat through the meeting, surreptitiously grading pop quizzes.

He'd paid just enough attention to jot down the new rules for answering the phone. He wanted to know what they were because the president had a habit of checking up. You never knew when he'd phone just to be sure people were giving the right response when they picked up the receiver.

But it wasn't the president. It was the dean's secretary calling back.

"Please hold for the dean," Melva said,

and Burns said he would.

Within a second or two, Dean Partridge was on the line.

"This is Dr. Partridge. Didn't your secretary tell you that I'd called?"

"She did, but I just got out of class," Burns told her. "I was reaching for the phone when it rang."

"Very well. I want you to come over to my office. There's someone here who wants to meet you."

Burns would have asked who it was, but he knew better. Deans never gave out information like that. They preferred to keep you in the dark, to make you wonder what was going on. It was part of their plan to drive the underlings crazy.

"I'll be right there," Burns said, thinking that he'd at least have an excuse to stop by and say hello to Elaine on his way back. Seeing her would make the whole trip worthwhile, no matter who was in the Dean's office, or at least that's what Burns told himself.

He told Bunni where he was going and left, hoping he wasn't going to meet a set of irate parents who wanted him or one of his faculty members fired for some act of atrocious behavior, such as failing one of their children or telling one of those same children that an instructor had a perfect right to require that they arrive in class on time.

When Burns got to the dean's office, he got a surprise. Melva Jeans told him to go right in. Burns tried to remember the last time a dean hadn't kept him waiting. He couldn't think of a single time, so he knew something odd was going on. He opened the door and stepped into the office.

Partridge was sitting behind her desk. She stood up and said, "Ah, here's Dr. Burns now."

A woman was sitting in one of the incommodious leather chairs. She turned and looked at Burns as he entered.

He saw that it was Mary Mason, and she gave Burns a friendly smile. She was made up to perfection, no doubt entirely with products from the Merry Mary line. Burns had no idea what her age was. It could have been anywhere between forty and sixty. He'd need to see her without the make-up to get a better idea. She wore a tight-fitting dress that showed off her impressive bosom, and lots of jewelry. It seemed to Burns that she had a ring on every finger. Her blonde hair looked like lacquered cotton candy, as if it might shatter if someone hit it with a softball bat, which Burns had no intention of doing, of course, though it made for interesting speculation.

"Have you two ever met?" Partridge asked.

"No, I don't believe I've had the pleasure," Mason said, standing up gracefully and smoothing her dress.

Burns was impressed by the way it clung to her hips, and he said, "I've heard a lot about you."

He didn't say what he'd heard. He didn't think she'd want to hear that Dr. Partridge thought she was capable of anything.

Mason extended her hand, and Burns took it. She had a firm, dry grip.

"I hope everything you've heard has been good," she said.

"Naturally," Burns said. A little white lie, but who was to know? "You're a good friend of the college, and that always counts for a lot with everyone around here."

Mason laughed. "*Good friend* means I give a lot of money, so it should count for a lot, all right."

Burns had no idea what to say to that. Partridge did. She told him to sit down. He did. So did Partridge and Mason.

Burns wanted to ask what was going on, but he knew better than that. Dr. Partridge seemed ill at ease, which was unusual for her, but he assumed it was because of her dislike for Mary Mason, who didn't look uncomfortable at all. She looked as composed as if they had all met for lunch at some fancy tearoom. Not that there were many tearooms of any kind in Pecan City, fancy or not.

For a few awkward seconds, no one said a word. Then Dean Partridge said, "Ms. Mason came to talk to me about something, and I wanted you to hear it."

"Hear what?" Burns asked.

"About the soldiers," Mary Mason said.

Chapter 17

"What soldiers?" Burns asked, pretending ignorance, which came naturally to him, and innocence, which didn't.

"You're a kidder, aren't you?" Mason said, reaching out to touch his hand. "I like that in a man."

Burns had the impression that she liked pretty much anything in a man. He said, "I'm not kidding."

Mason looked at Dr. Partridge, who shrugged.

"You tell him," Mason said.

Partridge did. "Ms. Mason came in this morning because she heard some story about a toy soldier, *my* toy soldier, being found beside the body of Matthew Hart."

Burns thought that over. He'd asked Napier who knew about the soldiers. It had been a short list, and Mary Mason wasn't on it.

"Where did you hear that rumor?" he asked.

"Rumor? I knew you were a kidder. It's no rumor. What I want to know is, did Gwen here kill old Matthew?"

Dean Partridge's lips thinned almost to invisibility. Whether the reaction was a result of the use of her first name or the implication that she might have had a hand in Hart's death, Burns couldn't tell.

"Dr. Partridge didn't kill anybody," Burns said. "And where did you get your information about the soldier?"

"Information. I like that better than rumor. Let's just say that keeping a secret in Pecan City is about as easy as putting on pantyhose in a steambath and let it go at that."

Burns didn't want to let it go at that, but he could see that what he wanted didn't make much difference. Mary Mason was used to getting her way, and she was going to get it this time, too.

"I know Gwen didn't kill Matthew," Mason went on, smiling at Dr. Partridge, who tried to smile back without much success. "I just like to see how people react when I say shocking things." She turned to Burns. "You're very cool and calm, you know?"

She touched Burns's hand again. Burns didn't think of himself as being cool and calm. He was feeling a little warm, to tell the truth.

"But you did want to say something about the soldiers?"

"Yes. You can tell him, Gwen."

Partridge looked as if she'd swallowed something nasty, but she didn't argue. She said, "Ms. Mason —"

"Please, Gwen. Call me Mary."

"Of course." Partridge swallowed. Hard. "Mary seems to have seen someone looking at my soldiers with real interest when she was at the party for the honor students."

"Then she should call the police," Burns said, feeling virtuous. "When you have information that pertains to a crime, you don't call an English teacher."

"I don't want to get involved in murder," Mason said. "Or even the petty theft of some toy soldiers. And I don't want Gwen and the college involved any more than necessary in either of those things. That's why I came to her. She's the one who called you."

"Dr. Burns is working with the police on the case," Partridge said.

Mason gave her a sidelong glance. "I understand that you work very closely with the police, too."

Partridge was sitting at her desk, her hands resting in front of her, fingers entwined. Her hands clenched together into one big fist, and Burns thought that she'd like to use it on Mary Mason's hair. Or maybe her face.

"I've been questioned about the theft of the soldiers," Partridge said, squeezing the words out with an effort.

"I hope Boss Napier didn't use any of his famous interrogation techniques."

Burns waited with interest for Partridge's answer.

"He was very . . . gentle," she said, and Burns smiled. Score one for the dean.

"Yes," Mason said. "He can be that way sometimes."

Okay, Burns thought, *call it a tie*. He said, "We seem to be forgetting about the soldiers."

Both women looked at him as if surprised to see him. It was as if he'd just wandered into the office off the street.

"Well?" he said, not letting their looks bother him.

Partridge took a deep breath and let it out slowly. "Ms. Mason, uh, *Mary* says that she and Steven Stilwell arrived at my house at about the same time for the party. Neither of them remembered the instructions about going directly to the back yard. The young woman who was directing traffic —"

"Bunni," Burns said.

"Yes, Bunni. Bunni told them they could

go right on through the house and outside, but Mr. Stilwell was so interested in the soldiers that he didn't want to go immediately. Isn't that right, uh, *Mary?*"

"Yes. Stevie said he'd be out in a minute. He just wanted to look at something first."

Stevie? Burns thought. *Stevie?*

"The young woman showed me on outside," Mason said. "But Stevie stayed behind to look at the soldiers."

"You're sure it was the soldiers he was looking at?" Burns said.

"I'm sure. He said something about them to me as we were going in the door, but I don't remember what."

"So he was in there with them alone for a while?"

"That's right, all alone. There was a very formidable young man with . . . did you say her name was Bunny?"

"Yes. With Bunni with an *i.*"

"How . . . cute. Anyway, the young man helped Bunni show me out. He was quite handsome, as well as large."

"His name is George," Burns said. "He's a football player."

"I could tell he would be good at . . . sports," Mason said, smoothing her dress over her thighs. Burns thought she might have licked her lips if she'd been alone.

"Are you good at sports, Dr. Burns?" Mason asked, looking at him with eyes that were a deep blue.

Burns blinked and thought about the softball game that was fast approaching. "Call me Carl. I play softball for the faculty team. We have a game on Saturday."

"Well, well. Maybe I'll come and watch. Will there be refreshments?"

"Never mind about the softball game," Partridge said. "We're here to talk about the soldiers."

"I seem to recall that Carl has been quite a help to the police in the past," Mason said, "though Boss Napier often gets all the credit. I hope that you can do something this time, Carl, before the college's good name gets dragged in the dirt."

"This doesn't involve the college," Partridge said. "Nobody here killed Hart."

"I'm sure Carl will find that out for sure," Mason said. "Isn't that right, Carl?"

"I don't now about that," Burns said modestly, feeling like a fool. If he'd had a forelock, he would have tugged it.

"He'd better," Partridge said. "And I'm sure Mr. Stilwell wasn't involved, either."

"How can you be so certain?" Mason said.

"Simply because he seems like a very

trustworthy person."

"You're not a very good judge of character, then, are you? I wouldn't put anything past Stevie."

Burns thought that Mason felt about Stevie the way Partridge felt about Mason.

"Dr. Burns will have a talk with him and clear this up today," Partridge said. "Isn't that right, Dr. Burns?"

It wasn't a question, but Burns answered. "I'll go by his place at noon."

"Do you have any other classes this morning?" Partridge asked.

"Yes, at ten o'clock." Burns looked at his watch. "I have to go get my things together pretty soon."

"You can go now. But don't wait until noon to talk to Mr. Stilwell. I want this cleared up."

"Fine," Burns said, rising awkwardly from the chair. He didn't have any idea that he could clear things up, but he was willing to say anything to escape the present conversation.

"I'll go downstairs with you," Mason said. She rose from her chair much more gracefully than Burns had managed and took his arm.

"Er," Burns said, and for the first time that morning, Partridge smiled.

★ ★ ★

There was an elevator in the building, but it was very old and very slow, and even though they would be going down only one floor, Burns didn't want to be alone in it with Mary Mason. He was beginning to get an idea of what Dr. Partridge had meant about her being capable of anything. So Burns started for the stairs.

Mary Mason had other ideas. "I sprained my ankle the other day, and I still don't do well on stairs. I know it's only one floor, but could we take the elevator?"

What could Burns say? He led the way, and they stepped into the tiny cubicle. When the steel doors slid shut, the elevator started with a shudder. Mason stumbled slightly, and Burns reached to steady her. Somehow they wound up with her leaning against him and his arms around her. Burns tried to disentangle himself, but he seemed only to make matters worse. He got the distinct impression that Mary Mason wasn't helping things any, and when the elevator shook to a stop and the doors slid open, they were still grappling in confusion, or at least Burns was confused. He was pretty sure that Mason knew exactly what she was doing.

It wouldn't have been so bad if Elaine Tanner hadn't been passing by just at that

156

moment. She glanced into the elevator, turned her head to go on, then did a double-take and looked back at Burns, who had by then gotten himself free and put a couple of inches between himself and Mary Mason.

"Good morning, Carl," Elaine said in a voice that would have put frost on a glacier. She went on toward her office without a backward look.

Burns started to follow her, but he found himself tripping over Mason's leg, which had in some way gotten between him and the open automatic door. Which started to close.

Burns made a desperate lunge, clearing Mason's leg and getting his hand on the leading edge of the door in time to stop it. He stood there holding the door and panting.

"You seem short of breath," Mason said. "Are you sure you're a softball player?"

"Not much of one. Excuse me. I have to talk to someone."

"Is it that little redhead? She's cute, but she could use a few make-up tips, not that I'm going to give her any. You could do a lot better, Carl."

The elevator door was straining against his hand. Burns let it close behind him as he started after Elaine. He thought he heard Mary Mason say something like, "Well, I never!" but he couldn't be sure. The door closed before she got it all out.

Burns sat at his desk and looked out his office window. There was a hill in the distance, dusty brown like a camel's back, with a narrow silver ribbon of highway running down the middle. At the foot of the hill there was a white square that had formed the screen of the drive-in theater. The theater had closed years before, but the screen was still there, a reminder of how things had been a long time ago. Probably not a single student at HGC had ever been to a movie at a drive-in. Most of the faculty hadn't, either.

Bunni had left, and Burns was alone in the office. His world literature class hadn't gone well. One of his students had complained that the stories they were reading didn't have any sex in them.

"We might as well be reading kids' books," the student said. "This G-rated stuff is boring."

Burns tried to explain that there was more to life than sex, though he refrained from mentioning that he was basing his answer on personal experience. The look on the student's face let Burns know that he knew, however.

Even though the class had gone badly, it had been a delight compared to Burns's conversation with Elaine, who might as well have been as far away from him as the hill or the screen of the drive-in. She had shown little interest in his protestations of innocence, and he had to admit it must have looked bad, what with him and Mary Mason wrapped around each other like eels in a basket. Nothing Burns could say could coax a smile from Elaine, whose main theme was something along the lines of "How could you?" and "That woman is capable of anything."

Burns supposed it was nice to know that Dean Partridge and Elaine agreed on Mary Mason's character, but it was small comfort to him. It was a little after eleven, and he was supposed to go see Stilwell about the soldiers, but he didn't feel like seeing anyone. He picked up the telephone and punched in Mal Tomlin's number.

"Tomlin."

"That isn't the courteous and proper way to answer," Burns said.

"Now ask me if I give a rat's ass. I'll tell you Burns, when a man's been shot at, his perspective changes. I know what's important and what's not, and answering a telephone courteously is in the *not* category."

Burns hoped that Mal wasn't going to be philosophical. Burns didn't need that right now.

"Let's have a smoke," he said. "I'll call Earl. We'll meet you in the boiler room."

"I'm on the way," Tomlin said.

Chapter 18

Although Napier had told Tomlin not to talk to anyone about the shooting, he had already told Fox, who found it hard to believe that he and Burns had been dodging bullets like a couple of extras in a Bruce Willis movie. But Burns assured him it was true, or sort of true.

"The trouble is that Mal had a routine," Burns explained. "The target of a killer should never have a routine."

"You mean I shouldn't walk the dog at the same time every night?"

"Exactly."

"But how was I supposed to know somebody wanted to shoot me?"

"That's a good question," Fox said. "Who'd want to shoot Mal?"

"That's exactly what I'd like to know," Mal said. "I'm a nice guy, never hurt anybody that I know of."

"Maybe a former student wants revenge," Fox said, taking a puff of the Harley-Davidson cigarette.

He was wearing a faded Hawaiian shirt and double-knit pants. Burns wondered if anyone made double-knit pants any more. He didn't think so.

"That's a possibility," Burns said. "Maybe the same student had it in for Matthew Hart."

"If that's it, he waited a long time," Tomlin said. "Hart's been retired for ten years."

"Probably not a student then," Fox said.

Burns nodded. "Maybe not. Can you think of anything else you and Hart might have had in common?"

"Who cares? Hart's dead, and I didn't much like him. I'm more worried about keeping myself alive."

"The murder is connected with you," Burns said. "Napier thinks that the killer is the same one who shot at you. If Napier can catch the killer, he'll have the guy who tried to get you last night."

Mal looked around the boiler room and puffed his cigarette. Finally he said, "Hart sold insurance. I bought a policy from him. I guess it's a good thing I did. You never know when your number's going to come up."

Earl laughed. "Your number's not up. Maybe it was just a jealous husband."

Mal gave a furtive glance in the direction of the boiler room door. "Don't say anything like that, not even in here. If Joynell ever thought I was messing around, she'd scalp me. Or worse. Nobody would have to shoot me in the dark. I'd be as good as dead anyway."

"You aren't messing around are you?" Earl said.

"Hell, no. I'd never do a thing like that. You should know me better than that."

Burns tried to get back to what interested him. "What about that insurance policy you bought from Hart?"

"I bought more than one policy. He had my home insurance and my car insurance, besides the whole life policy."

"I thought you didn't like him. I thought you said he probably screwed people who bought insurance from him."

"Yeah, but he taught in my department, and I thought I should throw a little business his way. Besides, he found some good rates for me. You don't think somebody is trying to kill me to collect insurance, do you?"

"Maybe Joynell is," Earl said. "How much are you worth?"

"Not enough for her to kill me. I hope."

"Do either of you know Steven Stilwell?" Burns asked.

Mal crushed the butt of the cigarette he'd

been smoking and lit another. "That guy who sells antiques?"

"That's the one."

"Joynell dragged me to one of the talks he gave here at the college. He explained the difference between Depression glass and pressed glass."

"What's the difference?" Earl asked, almost as if he cared.

"How the hell should I know? You think I paid any attention? Joynell made me come to the talk. I didn't give a damn one way or the other."

"I don't know him at all," Earl said. "I've never been to one of his talks or even into his store. He's supposed to be a big supporter of the college, though."

"What about Mary Mason?" Burns asked.

"Mmmmmmmmmm," Earl and Mal said in unison.

"Very good," Burns told them. "You should form a singing group. Or maybe a humming group. But that noise doesn't really tell me much about her."

"I just know that Joynell hates her," Mal said. "She's dated every eligible man in Pecan City and some of the ineligible ones."

"Not me," Earl Fox said. "And here I am,

as handsome a hunka hunka burnin' love as there ever was."

"She sticks to guys with money. That lets out anybody who teaches at HGC."

"Did she ever date Matthew Hart?" Burns asked.

"He was married," Mal said. "Very married. Not that a little thing like that would bother Mmmmmm."

Mason had picked up that detail about the soldier somewhere. Burns said, "Was she friendly with Hart's wife?"

"Women don't like her much," Mal told him.

Burns had noticed, but that didn't mean she wouldn't have gone by to pay a sympathy call on Mrs. Hart. Burns was willing to bet that's where she'd picked up the story about the soldier.

"Men like her," Earl said. "At least I do. Why are you asking about her, Carl? I thought you were pledged to Elaine."

"I thought so, too, until Elaine saw me and Mary in the elevator a while ago."

"Good grief!" Earl said. "And I thought you were a straitlaced kind of a guy, Carl. In an elevator, huh? How was it?"

"It's not what you think, and it's not what Elaine thinks, either. I'm just trying to get some information to help out the police

165

with Hart's murder."

"That's a good line," Fox said, nodding his approval. "I'd stick to it if I were you. Maybe Elaine will come to believe it eventually. In a decade or so."

"Who cares?" Tomlin said. "I have somebody shooting at me, and you two are worried about Burns's love life. Such as it is."

"Not me," Earl said. "Didn't Mmmmm go out with Stilwell for a while?"

"Probably," Mal said. "He's single, isn't he?"

"He hasn't always been single. I think he had a kid who went here a long time ago. I had him in class."

"Now that you mention it, so did I," Mal said.

"Stilwell doesn't look old enough to have had a son here a long time ago," Burns said.

"It was ten or twelve years. Anyway, Stilwell's around fifty-five. I think he dyes his hair."

"Now that's suspicious all by itself," Fox said. "He's probably your killer."

"Lots of people dye their hair," Mal said.

Fox looked closely at Tomlin's thinning hair. "Are you talking about anybody we know?"

"No. I was just making a comment."

Burns didn't think he was getting anywhere with them, so he said, "I have to go."

"You haven't had a smoke," Mal pointed out.

"I've quit again."

"You going goody-goody on us?"

"They just taste bad to me."

"Next thing, you'll start dyeing your hair."

"I don't have that much gray."

"You will if you keep on working here."

And if I keep on getting involved with Boss Napier's cases, Burns thought. He started for the door, then turned back.

"What happened to Stilwell's wife?" he asked.

"I don't know," Earl said. "It's not any of my business. Do I look like someone who'd pry into other people's business?"

"No, but then you don't look like a college professor, either."

"That was a low blow," Earl said, looking hurt and brushing cigarette ashes off his shoddy shirt. "I could afford to dress a little better if they'd only pay me more."

Burns didn't think Fox would dress any differently if he'd been paid ten times as much. Earl liked going to garage sales too much to change. The clothes weren't really the reason he went. He just liked the idea of pawing through the cast-off goods and getting a bargain of any kind.

Burns told them again that he was leaving.

"You going to lunch?" Mal asked.

"No. I'm going to look at some antiques."

"There are a couple teaching in my department."

"Not that kind," Burns said.

When he went out the door, Mal and Earl were lighting up again. The Surgeon General couldn't scare them.

Chapter 19

Stilwell's antique store was only a few blocks from the campus, so Burns decided to walk. It was depressing in a way. When Burns had come to Hartley Gorman College, Pecan City had been a bustling community, but the last few years had been devastating to the local economy. Downtown buildings that had been home to clothing shops and appliance stores were now mostly deserted. Someone had opened a used-book store in one of them. A spa had opened in another, but it had gone out of business within a couple of months. The work-out equipment had been repossessed, and the owner had absconded with all the membership fees he had been able to collect.

Stilwell's antique store was in an old building that had originally been a hardware store. It was one of the oldest buildings in town, and it was a perfect setting for the antiques.

Burns went in through the front door. He had never seen an actual puncheon floor, but the one on which he found himself standing was close enough. If it hadn't been made of planed and shaped logs, it was constructed of something similar. The old wood creaked when Burns walked on it. The stamped tin ceiling was high overhead, as high as the ceilings in the old Main Building on the HGC campus.

Stilwell was nowhere to be seen. Burns could hear low voices, and he assumed that Stilwell was with a customer in the back of the store, where they were hidden behind a wall that had once separated the business office of the hardware store from the sale goods. Stilwell had his own office back there, with most of the original furnishings still in place.

Burns didn't want to interrupt a business conference, so he stood and looked around the store. It was full of things that some people might have considered valuable collectibles, while others might have considered them nothing more than junk. Standing near a wooden counter on which a heavy cast-iron cash register rested, there was a wooden cigar-store Indian that looked almost new, and Burns decided that it probably was. He also thought that to be politically correct, he should think of it as a cigar-store Native American, and he did try, but somehow he couldn't get used to the idea.

On one wall there hung a number of clocks. One of the larger ones had a wooden frame and a glass front. The top half of the glass was clear, while the bottom half was painted black. On the black, in gold script, was an advertisement for Calumet Baking Powder. Burns could hear the clocks ticking and wondered if Stilwell wound them every day.

On the wall beside the clocks there were three free-standing cabinets with barred doors. The cabinets all held rifles, and Burns went over to look at them. The barred doors were locked, and there was a handwritten sign on each one that said "Military Rifles." Burns didn't know a military rifle from a BB gun, so all he could tell about them was that some looked different from others. There were several bayonets in the cases as well.

As little as he knew about military weaponry, Burns was nevertheless certain that a bullet fired from a rifle like one of those in the cases would never be mistaken for a .22 caliber such as the one that had killed Matthew Hart.

There were glass showcases all around the store, and Burns browsed around, looking in them. One of them was filled with costume jewelry that reminded Burns of the kind of stuff he'd seen on top of his grand-mother's dresser when he was a kid. Another showcase held watches of all kinds, and Burns walked over to check it out. Sure enough, on one shelf there was a Mickey Mouse watch like the one Burns had worn in the first grade. It had a cracked black leather band, and Mickey was missing one arm.

A free-standing bookshelf was in the center of the big showroom, and Burns went over to see if there were any interesting books in it. He didn't see any rare first editions, but there was a shelf of old paperbacks labeled "pulp fiction" on a piece of tape that was stuck to the shelf. Most of the books were at least forty years old, and Burns pulled out a couple to look them over. They weren't really what he would have considered pulp fiction, but he had to admit that they had colorful covers, most of them featuring women in various stages of undress. They had a different idea of how to sell books in the old days, Burns thought, and it wasn't exactly politically correct. It wouldn't have gone over well at HGC.

He put the books back and wandered over to another showcase that had old periodicals stacked on top. There was a pile of *Life* magazines from the 1950s, and Burns thumbed through them, finding the advertisements at least as interesting as the photographs that accompanied the sparse text of the articles. There were some comic books as well, but they were locked inside the showcase. Burns saw that on the top shelf there were several 3-D comics, including one with the Three Stooges on the cover. A note beside it said "Glasses still inside."

By now about fifteen minutes had passed since Burns had entered the store, but he continued to hear the low voices from the back room. He wondered if Stilwell was having difficulty closing the sale, or if he was just engaged in friendly conversation. Burns drifted in the direction of the voices, looking idly at the things he passed: stacks of old baskets and baking tins, metal advertising signs, racks of what a small paper sign referred to as "Retro Clothing," wooden toys, old plastic radios, cases of glasses, bowls, pitchers, and plates.

Some plates were probably pressed glass, Burns thought, and some Depression glass, but he hadn't attended Stilwell's lecture on how to distinguish between them.

One corner of the big store was given over to antique furniture, and Burns looked at a canopy bed and several chairs that appeared even more uncomfortable than those in Dean Partridge's office.

So far, Burns was not impressed. He'd been in the store before, and he'd never seen anything that he thought he couldn't live without. He supposed that he didn't understand the collector mentality, and he certainly didn't see why people would drive from Dallas or Houston to shop among Stilwell's admittedly abundant accumulation of seemingly worthless items.

Burns was wondering about it when he heard a short burst of maniacal laughter from the back room. It was loud and frightening, and Burns turned in the direction it had come from. It wasn't repeated, but Burns decided it was time for him to have a look in the office. He threaded his way past more of Stilwell's hoard, and when he came to the office, he saw that the door was half open. He knocked on the facing.

"Come on in," a voice called, and Burns went inside.

Steven Stilwell was sitting at a roll-top desk in an old wooden swivel chair on rollers. He was reading a tabloid that Burns could see was called *The Antique Trader*. There was no one else in the office, but sitting on a small table near the desk there was a nearly new compact stereo unit, from which had come the voices that Burns had been hearing. At the moment an organ was playing some very odd-sounding music. Stilwell laid down the paper and turned off the stereo.

"I was listening to an episode of *The Shadow*," he said. "One of the episodes that Orson Welles starred in. He was the best Shadow, don't you think? And the shows he was in are more like the magazine stories."

Burns had to admit that he didn't really know much about the Shadow. He'd read about the program and about the pulp magazine stories, of course, but he was far from an expert.

"Well, you should know more," Stilwell said. "Great show. And that laugh of his is priceless." Stilwell did a lame imitation of the spooky laugh Burns had heard earlier. "Who knows what evil lurks in the hearts of men?"

"Boss Napier," Burns said.

Stilwell leaned forward a bit in his chair and gave a more genuine laugh. He was thin, with a scraggly beard and long hair. Napier would have called him a hippie. He wore glasses with very small lenses, and his hair was black with a good bit of gray mixed in. Mal had been wrong about the dye job.

"Napier couldn't find his fanny with a

flashlight," Stilwell said. "And if you think he knows anything about human psychology, he really has you fooled."

"I wouldn't be too sure about that," Burns said. "He might surprise you."

"I doubt it. He wouldn't know a Marx character figure from a cheap Hong Kong knockoff."

Burns knew that Stilwell was wrong, but he didn't think it was worth arguing about.

"What brings you to my humble establishment, anyway, Dr. Burns? You didn't come to talk about Boss Napier and Old Time Radio, I'm sure."

"I was just looking around. You have an amazing assortment of odds and ends out there."

"You aren't interested in buying anything, though, are you?"

"How would you know that?"

"Because you hardly ever come around to look. People who collect antiques like to come in every week or so just to see what's new. They never know when I might have located something they need."

"Need?" Burns said.

"That's right. They need the things I sell just the way a drug addict needs his dope. Don't ask me to explain it. That's just the way it is. And I'm glad. It's how I make my living, after all."

Burns had talked to Stilwell on the campus a few times, but he'd never thought of him as a cynic. He said, "Some of that stuff out there looks as if it might be hard to sell to nearly anybody."

"It's that *nearly* that makes the difference," Stilwell said. "I believe in what I call the 'one sucker theory' of selling antiques."

"I don't think I know that theory."

"It's simple. If you're selling something, you just have to find the one sucker who wants what you have. You take that wooden Indian out there, for example."

Burns didn't want to take it and said as much.

"I know you don't want it," Stilwell said. "Hardly anyone would. It's not even an antique. But somewhere there's one sucker who wants it. Sooner or later, that one sucker will come into my store, and I'll make the sale. That's all it takes."

"What if that one sucker never shows up?"

"I wouldn't know. He always does. Eventually."

"You don't seem too busy right at the moment."

"Noon is always a slow time during the week. I come back here to the office and eat a sandwich while I read a magazine and listen to an old radio show."

Burns saw a sandwich bag, empty except for a few crumbs, on the desk beside a plastic Vanilla Coke bottle.

"What about toy soldiers?" Burns asked. "Ever get any calls for something like that?"

Stilwell leaned back in his chair and put his feet up on the desk. He crossed his arms and said, "So that's what this is all about."

Burns said he didn't get it.

"Oh, yes you do. I know all about those soldiers that are missing from Gwen Partridge's place, and since I'm the antique dealer, naturally I'm the suspect. Well, I didn't take them. They're nice items, and I could probably sell them."

"To someone like Neal Bruce, maybe."

"Maybe. He likes soldiers, and I've found a few for him here and there. He doesn't collect Britains, though. He goes for Staddens, which is another thing entirely. Maybe not to you and me, but to him."

"So you were definitely interested in Dr. Partridge's soldiers."

"You could say that. I even tried to buy them once. But I didn't take them. Be logical, Burns. Stealing them wouldn't be worth the risk. Why ruin my reputation for a few thousand bucks?"

"Mary Mason seems to think you were pretty fond of them."

"A-ha," Stilwell said.

Burns didn't think he'd ever heard anyone say that before. Maybe it was something Stilwell had picked up by listening to Old Time Radio.

"You know what they say about women scorned?" Stilwell asked. "Hell and fury and all that?"

"I've heard about it," Burns said, thinking about the way Elaine had acted after she'd seen him and Mason on the elevator. And he hadn't even spurned her.

"Mary Mason and I dated for a while. That was some time ago, and we didn't hit it off. I was the one who decided to call it quits. That's probably the first time that's ever happened to her. She's usually the dumper, not the dumpee. So she's never forgiven me."

"She called you Stevie."

Stilwell's mouth twisted in his beard.

"I thought it was sweet," Burns said.

"I don't, but it's typical. That woman is capable of anything."

Stilwell didn't seem to like Mason as much as other men did, Burns thought, *but then maybe that was because he knew her better than they did.*

"She was probably just covering up, anyway," Stilwell continued. "She may have taken them herself. She had an affair with Matthew Hart years ago, and she might even be the one who killed him."

"What does Matthew Hart have to do with this?"

"Nothing. I was just talking out of turn."

He knows about the soldier, Burns thought. But then so did Mason. Probably everybody in town knew.

"Why would she have killed him?" Burns asked. "An affair she had with him years ago doesn't seem like much of a reason."

Stilwell nodded. "You're right. I was just being vindictive. Forget it."

"All right. But what about the soldiers? Was she really looking at them?"

"Hell, no. I was. I always like to look at them. They're valuable, and they're well made. I admire good workmanship. But I'd never take them."

"Were you alone in the room for a while?"

Stilwell thought it over. "I might have been. I don't remember."

He could have taken the soldiers, Burns thought. There was no one else in the room, and he could simply have stuck them in his pockets. They were small, and no one would have noticed.

"How well did you know Matthew Hart?" Burns asked.

"What does he have to do with this?"

"You're the one who mentioned him."

"Oh. Yeah." Stilwell paused. "Well, I have my insurance with him. Or I had it with him. I guess I have it with his wife now. She's going to take over the business, or so I hear."

Burns hadn't heard, but then he was always the last to find out anything like that. He wasn't plugged into the community the way someone like Stilwell was.

There was one other thing that Burns wanted to ask about. He said, "I didn't know that just anyone could sell firearms, but you have quite a few of them out there."

Stilwell tilted his chair forward and stood up. His eyes flashed with anger.

"That's right, I sell guns. And I have an FFL, too, in case you were wondering."

Burns didn't know what an FFL was, and Stilwell must have realized it.

"An FFL is a Federal Firearms License. As I said, I have one, and I don't sell to anyone who doesn't have the special 'Curios and Relics' FFL, either. I operate strictly within the law. And I don't steal."

"I was just interested," Burns said. "I

181

wasn't accusing you of anything."

"It sounded to me as if you were."

Burns decided that it was time to leave, but he didn't apologize again. As he turned to leave, he saw a photo of a woman on the desk near the empty plastic bottle.

"Is that your wife?" he asked.

"I don't have a wife," Stilwell said. "That's Penelope Ann Miller."

Burns had heard the name, and the woman looked familiar, but Burns couldn't quite place her.

"She played Margo Lane in the movie version of *The Shadow*," Stilwell said as if stating a fact that should have been common knowledge among all thinking beings.

"I don't think I've seen the movie," Burns told him.

"It's all right, but it's not as good as the radio show." Stilwell seemed to have calmed down a bit. He reached over to the little stereo set and popped out the cassette. "Take this with you and give it a listen. You might even enjoy it. No charge."

"First one's free, kid," Burns said. "Is that it?"

"I don't sell radio shows," Stilwell said, "but it's not a bad idea. In fact, I think I'll order some and put them out by one of the old radios. It will make a nice display, and there might even be a market for them. Thanks for the idea."

Burns thanked Stilwell and stuck the tape in his pocket, but he didn't think he'd ever listen to it.

Chapter 20

Burns walked back to the campus, entered Main, and walked up the stairs to his office. Bunni was working at the computer, and she greeted him cheerfully when he entered.

He went to his desk and organized some of his notes for the next day's class. Then he asked Bunni if she knew Steven Stilwell.

"I've been to some of his lectures on antiques," she said. "Someday I'm going to have a house full of antique furniture."

Burns was tempted to ask what George Kaspar thought about that, but he didn't. He didn't want to get George in trouble.

"So you remember that he came to that party at the dean's house?"

Bunni thought it over a while before saying, "Yes."

"How about Mary Mason?"

"Oh, I know her. She's a real success story, a truly independent woman. She's made so much money selling cosmetics that she's practically a legend in Dora Hall."

Dora Hall was the name of one of the women's dorms on the HGC campus.

Actually the full name of the dormitory was Dora Hall Hall, since it was named for Mrs. Dora Watkins Hall, a woman that a former college president had once hoped would give a generous donation to the school. Unfortunately, Mr. Hall had outlived his wife, remarried, and moved to Maine, where he forgot all about any connection he might have had to Texas and Hartley Gorman College. The name of the dorm had never been changed, mainly because no other likely benefactors had come along.

"So the students here look up to Mary Mason?" Burns said.

"Not all of them," Bunni said.

Burns didn't ask why. He could tell from Bunni's tone that there were some things about Mmmmm of which even Bunni didn't approve. Even an independent woman could get away with only so much.

"I think I'll give her a call," Burns said.

Bunni gave him a startled look. "Dr. Burns!" she said.

"It's business," Burns said, smiling, glad he was still able to shock Bunni. He'd thought he was probably far too old for that.

He looked up Mason's number in the thin Pecan City phone book that he kept in a desk drawer and called.

"This is Mary Mason, and I sell Merry

185

Mary. How may I help you?"

Now there's a woman who knows how to answer a telephone, Burns thought. *Dr. Partridge could have hired her to give us instruction.*

"This is Carl Burns," he said.

"Why hello, Carl. I'm so glad to hear from you. Is there something I can help you with?"

"There might be. I paid a little visit to Steven Stilwell this afternoon, and he tells me he didn't take those soldiers. He says you accused him because you don't like him."

"Why, that sorry — I beg your pardon, Carl. I almost let my feelings get the better of me. I don't think Mr. Stilwell is very gallant."

So it wasn't *Stevie* anymore.

"He didn't like being falsely accused," Burns said.

"You're taking his word? Everyone knows that he's a notorious liar."

They'd come a long way from *Stevie,* all right.

"He says you had an affair with Matthew Hart."

"Why, that no-good — I beg your pardon again, Carl. But I'm beginning to think you might not be nearly as nice as you seemed this morning."

"My students could have told you that," Burns said. "And while I'm disappointing you, I might as well ask why you and Stilwell broke up."

"That's none of your business, Dr. Burns," Mason said and hung up her phone.

Burns hung up as well, more politely than Mason had, he thought, and glanced over at Bunni, who was giving him a wide-eyed look.

"That wasn't like you at all, Dr. Burns," she said.

"You weren't listening in, were you?"

"No. Yes. I was. I know it was wrong, but you didn't ask me to leave the office, and I couldn't help what I heard. I never heard you talk like that before."

"Some people bring out the worst in me," Burns said. He had a feeling Mason wouldn't be attending the softball game on Saturday. "I'm going over to the library, and I won't be back this afternoon."

"All right," Bunni said.

Burns was determined to set Elaine straight about what she'd seen on the elevator, but she wasn't in her office. Burns didn't try to find her. He just went home, where he fixed himself a peanut butter sandwich for lunch. It was so good that he had another one. He told himself that walking up those stairs to his office every day would take the calories off in no time.

After he ate the sandwiches, Burns thought he might as well listen to the tape Stilwell had given him. He put it in his tape player and was treated to the maniacal laughter again. The episode was called "Caverns of Death," and Welles informed him that the weed of crime bore bitter fruit. Burns hoped that was true for the person who had killed Matthew Hart and shot at Mal Tomlin.

Burns found that he enjoyed the show in spite of its melodramatic excesses. When it was over, he got ready for softball practice. Or as ready as he could get. He didn't think he'd ever be really ready, not in the way Mal Tomlin and some of the others were.

As he pulled on his old running shoes, Burns thought again that he really should do something to get in shape, but he knew he wouldn't.

He drove to the softball field in his Camry and parked behind the backstop. The field was located in what the local newspaper often referred to as Pecan City's "industrial park," but the fact of the matter was that not a lot of industry was located in Pecan City.

There were a few large buildings scattered around it, but one of them was vacant, and the others were home to industries that Burns didn't really think produced big money for the town. One of them manufactured wire of some kind, and the other produced plastic flowerpots and similar items. Probably plastic lawn gnomes. Well, there was no law against that. There was a furniture-making plant that employed more people than the other two places combined, but even that one didn't have a large economic impact on Pecan City. Taken all together, however, the three of them did provide jobs the town needed, and there were a few smaller plants as well. Most of them could be seen from the softball field, thanks to the hilly terrain.

The industrial park had once, during the Second World War, been one of the largest Army camps in the country, and there were still signs of the old camp to be found. Now and then some rancher would even discover an old unexploded shell in the field where his cattle were grazing, and in the places where tanks had been serviced there were still concrete roads and grease pits. Most of the roads were now cracked and hidden by mesquite trees, but some of them were still passable, and generations of

Pecan City teenagers (and not a few adults) had changed their cars' oil in the grease pits without much regard for the damage the old oil would do to the environment if it spilled out into the pit.

A little creek ran through the industrial park and passed along just behind the softball field's outfield fence. There was a regular little woods of mesquite, pecan, oak, elm, and hackberry trees behind the fence, but it didn't hamper the game. Though a couple of balls had gone over the fence in batting practice, no one had hit one into the creek, much less far enough to have it get lost in the trees beyond.

Past the trees a vacant factory building stood on a little hill. To the left of it was the Pecan City golf course, and of course there were a number of pricey homes around the course, the kind of homes that teachers at Hartley Gorman College couldn't afford. Burns knew that the Balls, Harvey and Karen, who were on his list of toy soldier suspects, lived in one of the bigger ones, and he could see it from the parking lot.

The rest of the team was already on the field, and today Dawn Melling was pitching. Burns wondered how she could get her pile of black hair under a baseball cap, and when he went through the gate, he could see that she hadn't managed it. The cap was sitting amid the hair, which straggled out all around. Nevertheless, she still looked pretty good out there on the mound in her tight jeans and a white HGC T-shirt that was filled to capacity. She had worn the shirt to an earlier practice, and Mal Tomlin, who was not nearly as sensitive to women's issues as Burns, had suggested that the initials should be changed to HGD, at the very least.

"Come on, Burns," Mal called out from the infield. "Make it snappy. We need to give Dawn a little workout so the old soup bone will be ready for Saturday."

Burns was picking up the lingo faster than he was picking up any real baseball skills, so he knew that "the old soup bone" was Dawn's arm. He didn't think it would need too much work because he was confident that the student batters, at least the males, would be so distracted by Dawn's appearance that they wouldn't be able to hit anything smaller than a regulation NBA basketball. In Burns's opinion, Dawn was the faculty's secret weapon, and his real hope was that because of her flashy form there would be few balls hit in any direction, much less his.

Of course that wouldn't excuse him for

being a poor hitter himself, but he thought maybe the faculty wouldn't need more than a couple of runs if the student team didn't score any at all.

"You can bat," Tomlin told Burns when he approached the playing field.

Mal seemed a little jittery, and Burns didn't blame him a bit. Burns didn't think he'd be at baseball practice if he'd been shot at the night before as Mal had.

"You're holding us up," Mal said. "Come on. Get in the box."

Burns picked up the black bat he had used on the previous day. If Mal was a little snappish, who could blame him?

Abner Swan was catching again, and he slammed his fist into his mitt a couple of times. "Come on, Dawn," he said. "Throw it right by him."

Burns didn't think that would be hard for Dawn to do. Just about anybody could do it.

Dawn lobbed the ball toward the plate, and an odd thing happened. For the first time in his life, Burns could actually see the ball clearly. It seemed to move so slowly that it was almost as if it were floating toward him. Maybe those peanut butter sandwiches had improved his vision or his reflexes or something.

When the ball reached the plate, it appeared to hang motionless, and Burns just knew he was going to hit it a mile. He took a mighty swing, and the bat connected with a satisfactory smack.

The ball soared high over right field, and it was heading for the fence. Burns was so surprised that he almost forgot to run toward first base, but then he remembered that he had to run even if the ball went out of the park.

And it was definitely going out. As he trotted toward first, Burns saw Don Elliott turn to watch as the ball sailed over the fence.

Just as it did, Elliott seemed to stumble. His cap flew off, and then he pitched forward on the outfield grass. Burns heard a crack like the sound of a distant firecracker. He crossed first base and kept going straight into right field.

"Call 9-1-1," he yelled, hoping someone had brought a cell phone. "Call Boss Napier."

As he stepped onto the outfield grass, Burns heard something buzz by his ear, and then he heard again the crack of what he was sure must be a rifle in the distance. He looked at the old factory building, but he couldn't see anyone in it. The late afternoon sunlight reflected off the metal sides of the building and off the window glass that remained. The other openings were dark and empty. Burns kept moving.

When he reached Elliott, Burns could see blood on the speech teacher's head and on the grass. But Elliott wasn't dead. Burns could see his hand moving.

If Burns had been an expert in First Aid, he would have stopped to help, but he didn't think there was anything he could do. The paramedics would be on the way as soon as someone called, and they could do more for Elliott than Burns could. So could just about anyone else on the field.

So Burns kept going. He came to the chain-link fence. It was only about four feet high, but Burns knew he couldn't vault it. He'd just emasculate himself. So he stopped and climbed over it, dropping down on the other side.

He ran a few yards into the trees and saw the ball he had hit lying there. He gave it only a passing glance and went on to the creek bank. The creek was a small one, and the muddy water that flowed in it was never more than a couple of feet deep. Today it was more like six inches deep and not much wider. Burns clambered down the bank, stepped across the water, and scrambled up the other side.

He didn't really think he had much chance of catching up with whoever had shot Don Elliott, but he was certain that the shooter was in the abandoned building on the hill past the woods. So he kept moving. Maybe the shooter would stumble and sprain his ankle trying to make his getaway, and then Burns would have him. Unless Burns sprained his ankle on the way to the building.

Burns arrived at the edge of the trees without injury and looked at the rusting metal building. It was rectangular, two stories tall. Burns was facing the side. He could see no movement inside, and no one took a shot at him, so he jogged around to the end, where there had once been a wide metal door that slid open on a track. The door was gone now, and anybody could go into the building with no problem. In fact, the opening was so wide that a person could drive a Hummer inside if he had a mind to.

Burns didn't go in. He stood to one side of the door and stuck his head around to see if he could spot anyone or anything.

Light from the windows fell in long rectangles across the concrete floor. Burns had no idea what had been made in the building, but he could see what looked like old oil stains on the concrete. A long steel track bolted to steel supports was suspended from the ceiling, and at the far end of the track a short chain hung from a big pulley.

There was another, smaller, door at the far end of the building, and it was open as well, creating a slight draft. Birds had at one time nested in the broken windows, and a couple of feathers drifted through the light along with the dust motes.

The building had no second story, but there was a steel stairway up to a catwalk that led to a small enclosure of some sort. Maybe it had been an office.

Burns knew that he shouldn't climb the stairs. He knew that if he did, Boss Napier would chew him out for spoiling the crime scene.

So the smart thing would be to stay right where he was.

But if he did that, the shooter might get away. The building was open at both ends, so he could just walk downstairs and zip out the end opposite the one where Burns was standing, and there wouldn't be a thing Burns could do to stop him, not if he had a rifle.

On the other hand, if Burns went to the stairs and blocked the way, he might get shot.

There just wasn't a good choice. Burns

looked down at his legs, which had begun to sting. He saw that they had been scratched and scraped by tree branches and maybe a sticker vine or two. He hadn't noticed at the time. His arms were scratched as well. But it wasn't too bad. Not nearly as bad as a bullet would be. Burns didn't like to think of himself with scrambled brains. He thought about Don Elliott, but he pushed the thought away.

Most likely the shooter had left the building long ago, Burns thought. He'd shot Elliott, taken a shot at Burns for good measure, and then gotten out of there.

Or not. There was only one way to find out.

Burns stepped past the wall and entered the doorway.

Chapter 21

Burns's old running shoes made no sound on the concrete as he walked to the stairway, and other than Burns the only moving things in the place were the air currents created by the two open doors and the broken windows. Now and then a piece of a nest would float down from a window, and Burns got the feeling that he was as alone as he could be within the city limits of Pecan City.

Just as he thought that, a small lizard darted out of a crack in the concrete and scuttled into the shadows by the wall. Burns looked carefully, but the lizard wasn't carrying a rifle. So Burns didn't worry about him.

When he came to the stairway, Burns examined it to see if there were any signs that someone had climbed it that day. He couldn't tell, though he had no doubt that Boss Napier had a crime lab expert who could. That is, if Burns didn't obliterate the signs.

Burns stared at the enclosure at the top of the stairs. There was nobody up there, he told himself. And there was certainly no need for him to go up there and find out whether he was wrong. He could just stand where he was and block the stairway.

So that was what he did. He was still there when Boss Napier came through the wide door and called out to him.

"What's the story, Burns? You have our killer cornered?"

"Technically speaking, there's no corner where I'm standing," Burns said.

"You know what I meant," Napier said, walking over to join Burns at the foot of the stairs. "Is he up there?"

"I don't think so. He might have shot Don from there, though. Is Don all right?"

"For a man who's been shot in the head, he's doing pretty well. The bullet just grazed the top of his scalp. Blazed a pretty good trail down it and knocked him out. He bled a good bit. Scalp wounds always do. And he might have a concussion, but that beats scrambled brains any day. He'll be making speeches again before you know it, but he won't be playing any baseball for a while."

Burns agreed, and he was glad to hear that Don was going to be all right.

"I don't think we should go up there," Napier said, looking up the stairway. "We'll leave that to the evidence team. Not that they're likely to find anything. They didn't at the pharmacy. Our guy is being careful."

"I've been thinking," Burns said.

"Always a dangerous thing to do, especially for you."

"I have an idea. If you don't want to hear it, that's fine."

"You don't have to get huffy, Burns. You're supposed to have a sense of humor, remember. Barrel of laughs and all that."

"I didn't hear any jokes," Burns said.

"All right, all right. I'm sorry if I hurt your feelings. Tell me your idea. We're not getting any younger here."

"Now that's witty. I'm almost laughing now."

"Gimme a break, Burns."

Burns decided that Napier was right. He deserved a break. So he said, "I was thinking that you can see Harvey Ball's house from the softball field. It would be easy enough to walk down here across the golf course, climb up these stairs, take a shot at Don Elliott, and stroll back home."

"Not bad, Burns. I would have worked that out myself any minute now, of course."

"No question about that. Do you think it

could have happened that way?"

"There's a good chance it could. Elliott was like your friend Tomlin. He had a routine, too, didn't he? Softball practice every afternoon this week. Bad to have routines if you're a target."

Burns didn't bother to point out that Elliott, like Tomlin, had no way of knowing he was a target. Instead, he changed the subject.

"How did the shooter get across the golf course with a rifle?" he asked.

"Easy," Napier told him. "Put the rifle in a golf bag and who's going to notice? In fact, if you were careful, it might be that nobody would even see you."

"I should have thought of that."

"But then you're not a trained lawman. Anyway, right now it would probably be a good idea for us to go have a little talk with Harvey Ball."

"Us?" Burns looked down at his sweaty T-shirt and his scratched arms and legs. "I'm not dressed to go calling on a rich lawyer."

"Rich lawyer. Isn't that one of those things you English teachers call a redundancy?"

"You're not as dumb as you look," Burns said.

"Thanks. Now are we going or not?"

Burns nodded at the stairway. "What about up there?"

"I trust your instincts, Burns. You said there's nobody up there, and I believe you. We'll leave it to the evidence team."

"But what if I'm wrong?"

"In that case, I guess I'd have to shoot you."

"That's another joke, right?"

"That's for me to know and you to find out."

"I can never tell when you're joking," Burns said.

"I know. Keeps you on your toes, right? Anyway, here comes the team, so we can leave."

Burn saw three people coming in through the wide door. He couldn't tell anything about them. They were just dark silhouettes against the light.

"Come on, Burns," Napier said. "We don't want to waste any more time."

He started off toward the narrow door at the other end of the building, and Burns trotted after him. They were nearly to the door when Napier stopped, and Burns nearly ran into his back.

"Hold it," Napier said.

He was looking at something on the floor, and Burns followed his gaze. Right there in front of them, something was lying in a square of light from one of the windows.

"Is that what I think it is?" Burns said.

"I don't know. What do you think it is?"

"It looks like a toy soldier."

"Bingo," Napier said.

"He's taunting us, isn't he?" Burns said.

He and Napier were squatting down on the floor, getting as good a look as they could at the soldier without touching it.

"Us or the people he's shooting," Napier said. He stood up, and Burns was pleased to hear his knees crack. "He's a real smart-ass."

" 'Crime does not pay,' " Burns said, standing as well. " 'The weed of crime bears bitter fruit.' "

"What the hell?"

"The Shadow," Burns said. "Did you think it was Shakespeare?"

"See? I knew you had a sense of humor. And I knew it was the Shadow, too. I was just surprised you did."

"It seems to me the Shadow might have been wrong," Burns said. "I don't see you catching this guy."

"Us," Napier said.

"I don't see us catching him, either."

203

Napier didn't respond. He said, "Lampson! Get over here."

One member of the crime scene team separated himself from the others and walked over to where they were standing. Napier told him to check out the soldier and to be extra careful with it. Lampson said he would, and Burns and Napier went on out of the building.

The afternoon sun was getting lower, and on the golf course some sprinklers were spraying water on the greens.

"Not many players out today," Napier said, looking out over the course. "All the better for our pal, the sniper."

"I was thinking," Burns said.

"Not again."

Burns laughed to show that he had a sense of humor. Then he said, "I was thinking that maybe whoever's doing this didn't mean to kill Matthew Hart. Maybe it was an accident."

They started across the golf course, trying to avoid the greens and the sprinklers. Burns wondered if they should be looking for tracks, but Napier didn't seem interested.

"You mean you think he might have missed Tomlin and Elliott on purpose?" Napier said.

"That's right. Maybe he's not trying to kill people, just scare them."

"Are you scared?"

"No. But I think Mal is. And Don Elliott certainly should be."

"So should the rest of the faculty at the college. For all we know this guy's shooting at them randomly."

Burns didn't believe that. "They must have something in common. We just haven't figured it out yet."

"You," Napier said. "You're on the faculty. Finding that connection is your job."

"I'm an English teacher, not Sherlock Holmes."

"You aren't even Dr. Watson, but sometimes you get lucky. It's happened before. Maybe it will again."

"Or maybe not."

"We'll just have to see about that, won't we?" Napier led the way around a sand trap, not bothering to see if there were any footprints in it. "Listen, Burns, it doesn't do my ego any good to ask you for help. But you're in with the faculty at the college, and you know the board members. You can get things from them that I might not be able to."

"I don't know the board members. I hardly know the Balls at all."

"Did you know he was a gun collector?"

Burns stopped and looked at Napier. "No. I didn't know that. How did you find out?"

"I'm a cop, remember? I find things out. And he likes to tour Civil War battlegrounds."

"I did know that," Burns said, and started to walk again.

"Well, you won't be surprised to know he's interested in military weapons and that he collects rifles."

Burns didn't know much about the history of rifles at all, but he knew enough to say, "They didn't have .22s in the Civil War."

"That's right, Burns, they didn't. I didn't know you were a history major."

"Minor," Burns said. "If Ball has a .22, wouldn't there be a record of it?"

Napier laughed. "That's a good one, Burns. There are a hundred ways a man can get a .22 without leaving a trace. One of them is to have owned one for most of your life. Half the kids in Texas had .22s when Ball was young."

"Did you have one?"

"I'm not as old as Ball, but sure, I had one. I went out hunting with it, too, and nobody thought a thing about it."

"Times have changed," Burns said.

"Damn right they have, and not for the better. Come on."

They were at the edge of the golf course, and Napier was heading for the house that Burns thought belonged to the Balls.

"I'll take the lead," Napier said as they approached the back door.

"You're the cop," Burns said.

Napier nodded. "And don't you forget it," he said.

Chapter 22

The Balls had a nice back yard, Burns thought, with green grass shaded by tall pecan trees, a swimming pool, and even what appeared to be an air-conditioned storehouse.

"Should we go around to the front?" he asked.

"Might as well surprise them," Napier said. "They won't expect the cops to be at the back door."

"Cop," Burns said. "Singular."

"Cop and English teacher, then."

"Not exactly Starsky and Hutch, are we?"

"Not exactly," Napier said, "but sometimes you just have to go with what you've got."

He walked around the pool and up to a sliding glass door. He knocked on it hard enough to shake it in its frame.

"Lousy protection," he said of the door. "A good thief could have it out of there and be inside in about three seconds."

A tall, gray-haired man wearing a pair of cotton slacks and a white polo shirt came to the door and looked out. When he saw Napier, he unlocked the door and slid it open.

"What's going on, Chief?" he said. "Is there some kind of problem?"

"Guy just got shot over at the softball field. Maybe you know him."

"My God. Who was it? Is he dead?"

"Don Elliott. He's not dead, but he's hurt."

Ball appeared to recognize the name. "I hope he'll be all right. He teaches at the college, doesn't he?"

"Speech," Burns said.

"Don't you teach there, too?" Ball asked. "I've met you before, I think."

Burns stuck out his sweaty hand. "I'm Carl Burns. I teach English at HGC, and I've met you at some college function or another. I was playing softball with Don when he was shot."

"I can't imagine anybody being shot at the softball field. What does it have to do with me? Are you here because I'm a board member, or is it something else?"

"We think the shooter might have come this way," Napier told him. "You haven't seen anybody suspicious in the neighborhood, have you?"

"No. I've been busy." His eyes lit up with

enthusiasm. "Come on back and I'll show you."

Burns and Napier looked at each other. Napier shrugged, and they went inside. They followed Ball across the den and down a hall into what Burns thought had once been a bedroom. Karen Ball was there, and so were Ball's military rifles, hanging on the walls.

"Why, hello, Dr. Burns," Karen Ball said. "I haven't seen you for a long time."

When she had decided to go back to school and get a teaching certificate, Karen had discovered just as she was about to graduate that she needed one more English class. She had taken only a couple of courses a semester, and she had already been working on her certificate for five years.

She had asked Burns's advice and had wound up in his American literature section. She had been a very good student. She was short, dark, and intense, and she always read the assignments, unlike a lot of the younger students in the class.

But Burns could see that Napier wasn't interested in either Karen Ball or the rifles hanging on the walls. He was interested in the large table sitting in the middle of the room.

"How do you like it?" Ball asked.

"It's great," Napier said. "What is it?"

That was a stupid question, Burns thought. It was a table. And on it there were lots and lots of toy soldiers. Confederate and Union soldiers, it seemed, arranged on some kind of man-made landscape with buildings, trees, grass, and roads.

"It's the battle of Shiloh," Ball said, "or it will be when I get it all set up."

Burns tried to remember what he'd learned about that particular battle in his history classes, but he didn't need to worry. The Balls were more than happy to explain.

"It was the first really important battle of the Civil War," Karen said. "Have you ever visited the battlefield?"

Burns and Napier said that they hadn't.

"It's a very sad place," Karen said. "So many tombstones. So many."

"Probably more than twenty-thousand casualties, all told," Ball said. "There were well over a hundred thousand troops involved in the battle. I don't have that many soldiers for my set-up, of course. Look here."

He walked to the table and pointed out a strip of silvery blue that was plainly supposed to be water.

"This is the Tennessee River. Here's the

211

little town of Pittsburg Landing, and this is Shiloh Church. Right here is the Hornet's Nest, where the Federals established a battle line."

Burns thought Ball had things set up pretty well, if you considered that one of his soldiers equaled about a hundred of the real thing.

"The South used more than sixty-two cannons against the Hornet's Nest," Karen Ball said. "If General Johnston hadn't been killed, the whole course of the war would have been different."

Burns remembered that historians didn't have much respect for General Beauregard, who had taken Johnston's place. But he wasn't interested in re-fighting the Civil War.

Neither was Napier, who said to Ball, "I didn't know you collected toy soldiers."

"It's a new interest," Karen said. "Have you met Gwen Partridge, the dean at the college? I'm sure Dr. Burns knows her."

Burns grinned. "Not as well as the Chief," he said.

"Well, then, you know about her soldiers. We saw them when we visited her house, and we started thinking."

"Always a dangerous thing," Burns said, and Napier glared at him.

The Balls didn't notice. They were caught up in their enthusiasm.

"We'd both studied the Civil War," Ball said, "and we've visited all the battlefields. So we thought, why not set one up here and see how things played out? We can move the troops around, try different scenarios, see how things might have turned out differently if things had been changed. It's an interesting hobby, and educational, too."

And one that a lawyer could afford, Burns thought. His gaze went to the rifles on the wall as Ball went on about the battle and his plans for his recreation of it. There was a place in one rack where nothing hung.

"What goes there?" Burns asked, pointing to the empty space.

"Oh, nothing, really," Ball said. "At any rate, I don't have to worry about the Army of Ohio under Buell's command. My set-up is the way the battle was before they arrived. That's thirty-five thousand troops right there."

"There's a gun missing," Burns said, refusing to be distracted. "Did you lose one?"

Napier had been listening to Ball, but now he turned to see what Burns was talking about.

"I didn't lose anything," Ball said. "I took it to be repaired."

"How could it get broken hanging on the wall?"

"It wasn't a collectible rifle," Karen said. "It was Harvey's old gun, the one he had when he was a boy."

Burns gave Napier a look. "Was it a .22?"

"That's right," Ball said. "My parents gave it to me when I was twelve. We lived in a little town a long way from anywhere, and I hunted rabbits with it."

"Been doing any hunting with it lately?" Napier asked.

"No. There was something wrong with it. I took it to be fixed."

"Here in town?"

"No. I didn't take it, really. I should have said I sent it off."

Napier seemed to remember why he'd come there in the first place. He said, "And you haven't seen any strangers in the neighborhood this afternoon?"

"No," Ball said. "I told you. I've been in here since I left the office. Isn't that right, Karen?"

Karen hesitated for just a second before saying that it was right.

"Are you sure?" Napier said.

"Well, Harvey did go out for just a minute. He had to get something from the store."

"Ink for my printer," Ball said. "But I came right back here. Surely you don't think I shot Don Elliott."

"Did someone shoot Don Elliott?" Karen said. "When? Is he all right? I had him for speech when I went to HGC."

"Did you have Mal Tomlin?" Burns asked.

"Yes. I had to get certified to teach, and he's chair of the Education Department."

"What about Matthew Hart?"

"Yes. He was in that department, too. I took an ed. psych. class from him."

"I'd like to know more about that .22," Napier told Ball. "Like where you sent it."

"I have the address somewhere. I'll give it to you if I can find it."

"Find it," Napier said.

"I'll find it later." Ball's neck was getting red. "And now I think you'd better leave."

Napier started to say something to Ball, thought better of it, and turned to Burns. "Let's go," he said.

"I'll show you the way out," Karen said.

"We'll manage," Napier said. "Come on, Burns."

Burns followed him out of the room, down the hall, and out the sliding glass door.

"Why didn't you browbeat him a little?"

Burns asked when he'd closed the door behind them. "You browbeat me all the time."

"Yeah, but you're not a lawyer. If Ball's guilty of anything, I'm not going to screw up the case by talking to him here. I'll wait until I have all my ducks in a row."

They started back across the golf course. The sun was low in the sky, blazing behind a cloud bank. One thing about Pecan City, Burns thought. You got a great sunset every day.

"You think he really sent a rifle off to be repaired?" Burns asked.

"Maybe," Napier said. "If he did, then he'll let me know where it went, and I'll check it out."

"He could call the people he supposedly sent it to, tell them to back him up."

"You have a suspicious nature, don't you, Burns?"

"That's what comes of being an English teacher."

"Yeah. Anyway, you're right. He could cover himself. But if he's guilty, we'll find out."

"He has soldiers," Burns said.

"Not the right kind, though."

"But there's a connection. It's tenuous, but it's there."

"Tenuous. Now there's a word you don't hear every day. You really do have a good vocabulary, Burns."

Burns got the impression that Napier wasn't impressed by his reasoning. He said, "Did you notice the questions I asked Karen Ball?"

"Very subtle," Napier said. "No one would ever guess what you were getting at."

"She took classes from everyone who's been shot at, so at least it's a connection. And it's not tenuous."

"Maybe not. But how many people do you think there are who've had Tomlin, Hart, and Elliott for class?"

"Hundreds," Burns said.

"Right. So it's pretty tenuous if you ask me. Of course if you're right and it's important, then you should be worried."

"Why?"

"Because she took your class, too," Napier said.

Score another one for the Boss, Burns thought.

The investigating team was still on the job when Burns and Napier got back to the big metal building, but Napier didn't want to disturb them, so he and Burns walked on back to the baseball field.

They had crossed the creek and were nearing the fence when Napier stooped down and picked up the softball that Burns had hit.

"What's this doing here?" Napier asked.

Burns told the story of his first home run, the longest hit he'd ever gotten.

"I guess they forgot to come after it in all the confusion," he concluded.

"And you just ran right past first base and climbed the fence?" Napier said.

"That's right. I didn't get to enjoy my moment of glory, and I'm sure I'll never get a hit like that again. For me, it was a once in a lifetime thing."

"So you didn't run around the bases?"

"Of course not. Don had been shot. I wanted to help, and I wanted to catch whoever did it. Surely you don't think I'd run around the bases."

"You never know," Napier said.

"Well, you do now."

"That's right. I do now."

Napier touched Burns with the ball.

"What did you do that for?" Burns asked.

"I tagged you."

"I know that. But why did you do it?"

"You're out," Napier said.

Chapter 23

Burns was still steaming when he got in his car. His one big moment on the ball field, and Napier had taken it away from him. Napier had handed him the ball after tagging him, and Burns threw it into the floor on the passenger side, where it bounced around a few times before coming to rest.

"You'd have been out anyway," Napier had told him. "You left the basepath, and that's an out. When you play a game, you have to play by the rules."

"But I hit a home run!"

"Not exactly. It would've been a home run if you'd completed your trip around the bases, but you didn't do that. So you're out. But don't worry about it. It wasn't a real game, just a practice. So it doesn't really matter."

It mattered to Burns, however. His one big moment, and Napier had ruined it.

Napier had tossed him the ball. Burns surprised himself by catching it.

"Besides," Napier said, "nobody's going to know you were out except you and me.

Everybody's gone home, and all they'll remember is that you hit it."

"Shouldn't you have questioned them?"

"I had somebody here to do that. You know what?"

Burns had a feeling he didn't want to know, but he said, "What?"

"They might not even remember you hit that ball so hard. When somebody gets shot, people tend to remember that, not anything else that happened."

Burns knew that his measly little home run meant nothing compared to Don Elliott's being shot, but it rankled him that Napier was rubbing it in.

"I think I'll go to the hospital and see how Don is doing."

"They might not let you in, dressed like that."

Burns hadn't bothered to comment. He'd taken his ball and gone home.

Well, not home. He had gone to the hospital, where he didn't get to visit Elliott but where a duty nurse told him that Elliott was asleep and doing just fine.

Burns started home then, but he changed his mind and drove to the HGC campus.

It was almost six o'clock when he got there, and students were going into Main

220

for their evening classes. Burns knew that his appearance was undignified and not in keeping with the way a faculty member should appear to the students, but he was still angry with Napier and didn't much care what anyone thought about how he looked.

He walked up the stairs to his office, ignoring the curious looks that he got from the students, and shut himself inside. When he had caught his breath from the climb, he sat down at the computer and turned it on. In theory he had access to the records of every student who had ever attended HGC, as all of them were supposedly entered into a database that was part of the new and hugely complicated software the college had purchased. It was so complicated, in fact, that many of the faculty members had simply given up on ever learning how to use it. Burns had faithfully attended every training session and practiced diligently. Even so, he was only barely competent. But he thought he could at least look up Karen Ball's transcript and find out whose classes she had taken. He might even be able to find out more, though he didn't know what that might be.

He worried for about two seconds over the doubtful legality of what he was doing. As an instructor, he had a right to look at the records, he knew, but he was pretty sure he was supposed to do so only for academic reasons. However, he told himself that he didn't plan to tell anyone about what he might find, so it was all right to look.

But what if there was evidence that would lead to the person who had killed Matthew Hart and shot at two other instructors? Burns decided he'd worry about that later. He had to find the evidence first, and that wouldn't be easy, since he didn't even know what he was looking for.

He started with Karen Ball. It took him a while, but eventually, after navigating through several screens, he found her transcript. Her grades were generally very good, though she hadn't done as well in Tomlin and Elliott's classes as she'd done in Burns's American lit. She'd made a C in both sections. And she had flunked Hart's course in educational psychology. That was interesting, but it had been a long time ago. Besides, Burns saw, she had taken the course again, from Hart, and made a B, so there was no reason for her to be upset after so long a time, certainly not upset enough to start shooting people.

Burns drilled down through more and more screens and located the rosters for the classes Karen had attended. He saw that her fellow students had included Steven Stilwell's son, who had also flunked Hart's class. But then so had another couple of students. It must have been a bad semester.

Burns fooled around with the computer for another half hour, but he learned nothing of interest. He left his office and went downstairs. Everyone was in class, so no one saw him.

He thought about going home, but there was nothing there that he wanted to eat for supper, so he drove to the Whopper Burger and got a number six ("an old-fashioned burger, just the way your mother used to fix 'em") with fries and a soft drink. He found a space in a deserted corner of the parking lot where he could eat and think.

He didn't think much about the murder. Instead he thought about his home run that had become an out, thanks to the sneaky Boss Napier, and he thought about Elaine Tanner. Then he remembered why she hadn't been in the library that afternoon when he'd gone by to see her. The library staff took turns at working in the evenings, and when they did an evening shift, they got the afternoon off. Which meant that Elaine would be at work at that very moment.

Burns finished his burger, wishing he

hadn't gotten the old-fashioned one with onions, and washed it down with what remained of the watery soft drink. They always put too much ice in the drinks at the Whopper Burger, he thought. In fact, that was true of every fast-food place where he'd ever eaten. Maybe it was a way to save money.

He listened to the radio as he drove to the library, but the news on the all-talk station was depressing. Several more American troops had died in yet another helicopter accident in Iraq, and even though the war was over, the casualties kept mounting. He put in the Warren Zevon CD. Listening to Zevon sing about the werewolves of London was a lot more uplifting than hearing the news.

When he arrived at the library, Burns managed to get back to Elaine's office without being spotted by anyone other than the student at the check-out desk. He felt grungy, and the scratches on his arms and legs itched. The good news was that he'd found a package of breath-freshening strips in the console of the Camry and let two of them dissolve on his tongue, so his mouth no longer tasted like onions and mustard. He might not look the part, but he felt he was a fine candidate for a romantic reconciliation.

Elaine was at her desk, reading a book, and she looked up when he got to the door.

"What happened to you?" she said.

Burns told her about Don Elliott's being shot and his own run through the woods to look for the shooter. As it happened, Elaine had already heard about Elliott, although she hadn't heard about Burns's heroic attempt to find the person who shot him.

"So you were in real danger?" Elaine said.

Burns smiled modestly. "Not as much danger as I was in from Mary Mason in that elevator."

Elaine's look of concern turned to one of disgust. "I don't want to talk about that."

"But we have to," Burns said, blocking the doorway so that Elaine couldn't make a quick exit. "Believe me, it was nothing. Well, okay, it was something, but I didn't have a thing to do with it. I didn't grab her. She grabbed me."

"I don't believe that. She's a lady. She would never throw herself at a man."

"You must be the only person in Pecan City who believes that. And you should know me well enough to realize that I'd never try to make out with a woman in an elevator."

Elaine thought it over. After a few seconds she said, "That's true. And it's not one

225

of your most endearing qualities, if you must know."

Burns was taken aback. "You mean you'd like me better if I tried to make out with you in an elevator?"

"I didn't say that."

"Well, you implied it."

"Possibly. But we aren't anywhere near an elevator, are we?"

"No, but we're in your private office."

"It's not so private. People walk by here all the time."

"But they couldn't see anything if the door were to be closed."

"That's right, they couldn't. But as you can see, the door's wide open."

"Not for long," Burns said, stepping into the office and pulling the door shut behind him.

Burns felt much better when he left the library. Elaine was no longer angry with him, and he even wondered if she hadn't simply pretended to be in order to goad him into making up with her. It didn't matter to him, one way or the other. The making-up had been worth the anxiety he had felt.

On his way home, he drove by the Yowell Pharmacy. It was still open, so Burns parked in the lot and went inside. Yowell was on his list of suspects, and this was as good a time as any to talk to him. The element of surprise, as Napier would say.

The fluorescent lights in the pharmacy gave the place an icy brightness that Burns didn't much like. It gave an odd color to the scratches on his legs.

One of his former students, Ron Williams, was at the check-out counter in the front of the store. There were no customers in sight.

"Hi, Dr. Burns," Ron said, looking him over. "You need something to put on those scratches?"

Burns hadn't even thought about putting anything on the scratches. And he figured it was too late now. If they were going to get infected, they'd already done it.

"I'm all right," he said. "I was wondering if Mr. Yowell was working tonight."

"Nope. Mr. Lee's filling in."

Burns was immediately suspicious. "Is Mr. Yowell sick?"

Ron laughed. "I hope not. He and his wife drove to Galveston yesterday. They're going to meet his brother and go on a cruise over to Key West and then on down to somewhere in Mexico this weekend."

"Oh," Burns said. It sounded like the perfect alibi to him. If the person who had killed Hart was the same one who had shot at Tomlin and Elliott, Yowell was in the clear. "Well, I hope they have a good time."

"I'm sure they will. They've been looking forward to this for months. He said he really needed some time off. I hope what you wanted to talk to him about wasn't an emergency because he didn't even take his cell phone with him."

"It wasn't important," Burns said. "I can see him when he gets back."

He didn't plan to do that. There was no need for it now.

"Thanks for the help," Burns said.

"You're welcome," Ron said, and Burns realized he hadn't heard anyone say that for a while. These days when you thanked people, they always said "no problem" or "sure thing" or something similar. The language kept on changing. He supposed that was a good thing, but there were times when he didn't much like it. Probably that was a sure sign he was getting older.

It had been a long day, and Burns hadn't gotten much sleep the night before. It wasn't late, but he didn't feel much like doing any reading. He listened to the other side of the tape Stilwell had given him. It was as entertainingly melodramatic as the first side had been, and Burns was a little sad to think that once there had been a time when you could turn on the radio and hear shows like *The Shadow*, whereas these days you could run the AM dial from one end to the other and find nothing more than arrogant windbags expounding on their political views or would-be jocks giving their insipid "takes" on some sports team. The FM dial wasn't much better. Burns didn't like country music that sounded like pop tunes, he didn't understand the appeal of rap, and he thought most of the R&B music sounded like people moaning in pain. Another sign of his rapid aging, Burns thought.

He went to bed, but he couldn't sleep. He kept going over things in his mind, and he realized that one problem was that he still hadn't talked to all the suspects.

He told himself that questioning them was none of his business, no matter how much Dr. Partridge or Boss Napier pushed him. Napier or one of his minions had probably already tried to interview Yowell, for example, and nobody had mentioned to Burns that Yowell was out of town. You'd think they'd let him know things like that.

Burns thought about the other suspects, Neal Bruce and the Codys. All of them as rich as anyone in Pecan City. Richer, most likely. What possible motive could any of them have for stealing toy soldiers or shooting at HGC instructors? Sure, Neal Bruce collected toy soldiers, but there would be no need for him to steal any from Partridge. He could buy all her soldiers with his pocket change. The Codys could buy them with the change they found under their couch cushions. Thinking that they would steal them was ridiculous.

But that didn't mean it couldn't have happened.

Burns decided to let Boss Napier worry about it. He was tired of being involved. From now on, he was going to teach his classes and stay out of things.

When he finally got to sleep, he dreamed he was being chased through the woods by an army of tiny toy soldiers, some of them dressed in British uniforms and some of them wearing the blue and the gray of the Confederacy. All of them holding little softballs, all of them trying to tag him out.

Chapter 24

Neal Bruce looked exactly the way Burns thought a banker should look. He was middle-aged, silver-haired, and a little stout. Not fat, but just well filled out. His suit was expensive, and so was his haircut. His office was on the third floor of the Universal Bank Building, and it was paneled in unfashionable dark wood. But it was a corner office and had windows on two sides, so it was well lit and quite pleasant. There were tall cabinets on two walls, and they were filled with toy soldiers that Burns assumed were Staddens. Bruce himself sat behind a big wooden desk and asked what he could do for Burns.

Burns considered asking him to confess to Matthew Hart's murder, but he didn't think that would work. And he didn't know what would. He didn't really even know why he was there in Bruce's office. He certainly hadn't planned to be, but after his class that morning, he'd returned to his office and found Boss Napier waiting for him.

Napier had told him that while the crime

scene investigation had pretty much proved that the shot at Elliott had been fired from the old metal building the previous afternoon, there hadn't been anything else in the way of helpful evidence.

"The shooter is picking up his brass, and he's probably wearing gloves," Napier said.

Burns knew what *brass* was, but he pretended that he didn't.

"Empty cartridge shells," Napier said. "They should be there if they weren't picked up. So they were."

"So how do you know the shots were fired from there?"

"The toy soldier, for one thing. It's one of Gwen's. And there were footprints in the dust on the stairway and in the little room it led to," Napier said.

Burns mentioned that he'd been by to talk to Roy Yowell. "But he wasn't there. You probably knew that already."

"Sure. He and his wife are on a cruise. First thing I did was check on the whereabouts of all the people on Gwen's list."

"So there's no doubt that he's gone off into the Gulf of Mexico on a ship?"

"Not a bit. I've talked to his family, and I'm convinced he's there. He and Hart had their differences, that's for sure. But Yowell is mostly just bluster. Even at that he never made any threats. And he didn't have anything against Elliott or Tomlin, as far as we know."

"Neither did anyone else, as far as we know. And you should have told me about Yowell."

"I thought you'd rather find it out for yourself, you being such a hotshot investigator and all."

"I never said that."

"Yeah, I know." Napier's mouth twisted snidely. "Gwen's the one who thinks so, but don't let her know I told you."

Burns hadn't known that the dean had such a good opinion of him, though she was the one who'd asked for his help in the first place.

"I hope you're not jealous," Burns said.

"Nah. Not a jealous bone in my body. Besides, why would I be jealous? I don't have any interest in Gwen."

Burns kept a straight face. He said, "What about Elaine?"

"Now that's one good-looking woman," Napier said. "And I think she likes me. You aren't jealous, are you?"

"Not a jealous bone in my body," Burns lied. "But I have a feeling you didn't come here to talk about your amazing appeal to women."

"Nope. I came to ask if you'd talked to Neal Bruce yet."

"No, and I don't plan to. I've decided to stick to being an English teacher. This crime business is way too complicated for me."

Napier did a take. "You're kidding me, right?"

"No, I'm not kidding you. I'm not getting anywhere at all by talking to people. They're not telling me anything useful, and I don't need the aggravation."

"You think you have aggravation now?" Napier said. "Wait and see what you get from me if you don't talk to Bruce."

"Why do I have to talk to him? You can do that as well as I can. If you don't want to do it, send somebody else from the department."

"I've already talked to him. I didn't get anything out of him, but I think he's hiding something. You might be able to catch him off-guard."

"What makes you think so?"

"Because you teach here, and he's on the board. You can talk to him about college stuff, lull him into a false sense of security, and then pounce."

Burns tried to think of himself pouncing. The image just wouldn't come. He wasn't a pouncer, and he told Napier so.

"Give it the old college try, then, as a favor to me," Napier said.

"The old college try?"

"You know, like winning one for the Gipper. Don't you have any school spirit, Burns?"

"This isn't an athletic contest."

"Just try it. See what you can find out."

"I didn't find out anything from Stilwell."

"How do you know? You haven't told me what he said yet. Maybe there's something you didn't pick up on. Tell me the whole thing."

Burns told him what he remembered. He didn't think Napier had learned anything from the recitation, but that hadn't stopped him from wheedling Burns into talking to Bruce, which was why Burns now found himself in the banker's office, telling Bruce that he'd come there about the stolen soldiers.

"As a board member," Burns said, "you can understand that it wouldn't look good for the college if the word got out that our students were thieves. You were at Dean Partridge's party when the soldiers were taken, and she asked me to check with you to see if you'd noticed anything suspicious."

Bruce looked out a window while he

thought it over. He struck Burns as one of those people who always thought everything over before speaking, which sometimes resulted in long pauses in the conversation.

"No," he said, turning back to Burns, "I didn't see anything suspicious at all." He waved a hand at the cabinets against the wall to Burns's right and then waved to the left. "As you can see, I collect soldiers, too, and they're very well insured, let me tell you. And while those cabinets might look easy to break into, they're not. They're locked, of course, and that's not glass you're looking through. It's plastic, a very tough plastic. To get any of my soldiers, you'd have to take those cabinets apart. Believe me, it wouldn't be an easy job."

"Dr. Partridge could learn a thing or two from you."

Bruce thought about that. Then he said, "She's a good woman, but she's too trusting. She tends to believe the best of everyone, and that's not always a good idea."

Spoken like a man who'd made a bad loan or two in his time, Burns thought. He said, "She certainly thinks the best of Steven Stilwell."

This time Bruce didn't have to think. "I've had some dealings with him, and he's always been quite fair."

"He's sold you soldiers, I suppose."

"Yes, among other things. I have several collecting interests."

"You were in the military, weren't you?" Burns asked.

"Yes. That was a long time ago, though. Why?"

"I was just wondering why you collected the soldiers."

"Not because they remind me of my time in Vietnam, I can tell you. I don't want to be reminded of that. It was just as bad as you may have heard it was, and I'd prefer to forget it, not remember it. Those soldiers in the cabinets remind me of my childhood, which was a much happier time. I had a great childhood."

"Do you have any Britains?"

Bruce paused for quite a while and stared out the window. When he finally turned to Burns again, he said, "I hope you haven't come here because you think I might have taken those soldiers."

"Absolutely not," Burns said. He felt he was becoming quite good at lying. Associating with Boss Napier would do that for a guy. "Dean Partridge just thought that you might have noticed something, seen somebody alone in the room with the soldiers maybe."

"How could they have been alone if I saw them?"

"A poor choice of words on my part," Burns admitted.

"I'd say so." Bruce leaned forward. "I didn't take the soldiers, Dr. Burns, and I don't know who did. You have my word on that. I hope that's good enough for you."

Bruce leaned back in his chair, and Burns knew that he'd been dismissed. He stood up, thanked Bruce for his time, and left.

Standing in the hall, Burns thought that Napier must be wrong. Bruce hadn't seemed to be hiding anything. He was as forthright and straightforward as anyone Burns had talked to lately, and that certainly included Napier.

Burns glanced toward the elevator doors but decided to walk down to the first floor. He shouldn't pass up the chance to exercise. He walked down the hall and opened the door that led to the stairway. He was about to let it close behind him when he heard the elevator doors open. He turned his head to see who was arriving and saw Mary Mason step out of the elevator.

He concealed himself behind the door for a second, then peeked out again to see where she was going, which turned out to be Bruce's office.

Well, well, Burns thought. *Maybe Bruce does have something to hide, after all.*

Burns went on down the stairs, trying to figure out what was going on. There was probably a perfectly legitimate reason why Mary Mason was visiting Neal Bruce. She was in business for herself, and she would naturally need the services of a banker from time to time.

On the other hand, Dr. Partridge had said that Bruce was merely a figurehead and didn't have much to do with the actual banking these days. And he certainly hadn't looked busy while Burns was there. He got no calls, had no paperwork in sight, and in fact didn't even have a secretary.

So what was Mason doing there?

Burns couldn't come up with an answer.

By the time he reached the front door of the bank, Burns had decided to stick around and talk to Mary Mason when she left. He didn't want to lurk in his car, so he walked across the street to the little used-book store that was located where a men's clothing shop had once been. He looked over the mystery shelf while keeping one eye on the bank.

He'd pretty much memorized the entire contents of the mystery section by the time Mason emerged, but he hadn't found anything that he especially wanted to read. Just as he started for the door, he spotted an old Charles Willeford novel in the "collectibles" rack by the counter. It was a Beacon Book called *The High Priest of California*, and there was a "bonus" novel called *Wild Wives* in the same volume. It was priced at five dollars, which Burns thought was reasonable enough, so he bought it.

Unfortunately the delay had caused him to miss Mason. Her big pink Caddy was pulling away from the curb by the time he got outside. He jogged to his Camry, got in, and followed her.

Chapter 25

Burns had no idea where Mary Mason was going, but he thought she must be headed home. She went past the college, turned right, and started toward one of Pecan City's residential sections. But after a few blocks she turned left, turned left again at the next corner, and drove back toward town.

Burns followed at what he felt was a discreet distance. As usual, there wasn't much traffic on the streets, and he had no trouble keeping the pink Cadillac in sight. Following a car like that, he wouldn't have had any trouble if they'd been in Houston at the afternoon rush hour.

Mason went back through town, and when she came to the intersection where there had once been a traffic circle, she turned right on the highway leading out of town.

Maybe she was making her getaway. Burns was determined to follow her, no matter what. He had a feeling that he was making progress at last.

Boss Napier had obviously been right

about Bruce. The man had something to hide, all right, and Mason was the key to it. Burns would confront her and find out everything, or so he told himself. Maybe he wouldn't even have to confront her. Maybe she would lead him straight to the evidence that he was looking for.

What she led him to was the Pecan City Park. It was several acres of land on the bank of a wide creek. Mason turned in, and Burns followed.

The park was shaded by tall pecan trees. There were picnic tables scattered here and there, swings for the kids, and a jogging trail that wound through the trees and along the bank of the creek. Burns had heard that the high school students liked to come out to the park at night and drive to the more secluded areas toward the back of the acreage, where they would do whatever it was that kids that age did these days. Burns didn't think he wanted to know.

On the other hand, maybe he should give it some thought, as Mary Mason didn't stop at any of the tables, and she didn't appear to be there to get her exercise on the jogging trail. She was driving straight, or as straight as she could on the winding gravel road, to the back of the park.

Burns stopped his car. He couldn't go any

farther without making it painfully obvious to Mason that she was being followed, so he pulled off by the road beside one of the picnic tables and stopped to wait for her to return.

He opened the book he had bought, but he'd read only the opening sentence before it dawned on him that Mason might be meeting someone in the secluded area in the rear of the park. If that was the case, then Burns wanted to know about it.

He put his book on the seat and got out of the car. He couldn't drive back there, he thought, because Mason and whoever she was meeting would hear him coming. So he would sneak up on them on foot. Burns sidled through the trees, trying to conceal himself behind them as he made his way through the park.

It was cool under the trees, and Burns could hear the creek flowing nearby. There was no one else in the park, except for Mason, and she wasn't anywhere to be seen. Burns felt a little like Natty Bumppo, the Leatherstocking, slinking through the primeval forest in a James Fenimore Cooper novel.

After a couple of minutes of slinking, Burns could see the telltale pink of Mason's Cadillac, a sight the likes of which Natty

Bumppo had certainly never seen. The car was parked between two bushes near the point where the park ended at a tall chain-link fence. There was no way Mason could have gotten over the fence, so Burns knew that she was nearby. He just didn't know where.

He stood behind the thick trunk of a pecan tree and tried to see some sign that Mason had met another person. He didn't see anyone or hear anyone. He didn't see another car. He didn't even see Mason.

Well, she had to be there somewhere. Burns took a step forward and stepped on a rotten twig. As soon as he heard it crack under his foot, he thought of Natty Bumppo again, more specifically of Mark Twain's comment that the Leatherstocking Series should have been called the Broken Twig Series. Burns knew that he had announced his presence as carelessly as any of the inept characters in Cooper's books. Now all he could do was wait until a hostile Mingo came to take his scalp, such as it was.

But no one came for his scalp, not even Mary Mason, so Burns took another step or two in the direction of her car. He could see now that there was no one inside it, so Mason was meeting someone, somewhere. All he had to do was find them.

He stood behind another tree and listened for a voice. He still could hear nothing other than the sound of the creek, some birds, and a squirrel that was chattering not far away.

Using his suddenly acquired skill in the craft of the forest, Burns deduced that the squirrel was no doubt angry because it had been disturbed by someone who didn't belong in the park. So he started off in the direction of the chattering.

He hadn't gone far when he found Mary Mason. Or, to be more accurate, she found him.

Burns heard a movement behind him and turned just in time to see Mason's well-aimed handbag heading for his face at a high rate of speed. He wasn't quick enough to get out of the way, but he did manage to turn a little to the left, which was a good thing. Judging from the weight of the handbag when it hit the side of his head, he was pretty sure it would have broken his nose had it hit him there.

He staggered to the side, ran into a pecan tree, bounced off, and barely managed to duck under the handbag as it swiped at his head again. He wondered how Mason could handle it so easily. She wasn't a large woman, and he was pretty sure there was a bowling ball concealed inside the purse.

"It's only me," Burns said, which he knew was awfully lame, but he couldn't think of anything else.

"I know it's you, you slimy bastard," Mason said, swinging the purse at him again.

Burns dodged behind the pecan tree he'd bounced against, and the purse cannoned into the trunk. Burns was surprised that pecans didn't rain down all around him, but then it wasn't the season for pecans.

"You thought I didn't see you spying on me at the bank," Mason said. "But I did."

She made a feint to the right and Burns dodged to the left, looking at her from around the trunk. He didn't feel like Leatherstocking now. He felt more like Elmer Fudd facing a berserk Daffy Duck in some bizarre Warner Brothers cartoon.

"I wasn't spying on you," he said.

Mason leapt to the left, and Burns jumped back to the right. When he peered out from behind the tree again, Mason said, "You were spying. Neal told me all about it."

"What is it with you and Neal?" Burns said, and then he realized that he had just asked a very stupid question. Any woman in Pecan City, except possibly Bunni, could have told him the answer to that one.

"It's none of your business," Mason said, which didn't answer the question but which pretty much confirmed what Burns was already thinking. She hadn't been seeing Bruce about anything related to banking, that was for sure.

"Look," Burns said, "I feel like a fool. I'm going to come out from behind this tree, and I want you to promise not to hit me."

Mason looked almost disheveled. A few strands of hair had escaped the hive and were dangling in her face, and her make-up was streaked. He doubted that many people had seen her in that condition.

"I'm not promising you anything," she said, but she backed up a step.

Burns came from behind the tree, his arms spread, his hands open with the palms outward. It was, he thought, the way Natty Bumppo would have demonstrated to an irate Mingo that he meant no harm.

"I just want to tell you," he said, "that I know your personal life is your own business and that I don't mean to pry into it. It's just a coincidence that I saw you at the bank today."

Mason snorted. It wasn't a polite, ladylike little snort like heroines in romance novels gave when told something they didn't believe. It was a loud snort of derision.

"And I suppose that you followed me here to the park by coincidence, too," she said.

"Well, no, I have to admit that I did it on purpose."

"You're darned right you did, you little sneak. I have a good mind to report you to Gwen Partridge."

Burns relaxed a little. At least she hadn't threatened to report him to Boss Napier.

"Why don't you go ahead and call her?" he said. "That is, if you didn't break your cell phone when you bashed me in the head with your purse."

"I wish I'd bashed you harder, you little sneak."

Burns didn't think it would do any good to tell her he wasn't a sneak. Mainly because he was one, more or less. The fact that he was a sneak in the service of a good cause, or thought he was, didn't really excuse him, he supposed.

"You bashed me hard enough," he said.

"No I didn't. You're still walking and talking."

Burns was a little surprised at the intensity of her feelings. He wouldn't blame her for being a little upset with him, but she was more than a little upset. She was a *lot* upset. So naturally he wondered why.

"Is there some reason why you think you

have to keep your relationship with Neal Bruce a secret?" he asked.

"See? I knew you were spying on me, you little sneak."

"Minus ten for repetition and lack of originality."

"You — what?"

"Once an English teacher, always an English teacher. That's three times now you've called me a *little sneak*. You'll have to come up with something better than that."

Mason grinned. "All right. How about this: You scum-sucking pig."

"I'm afraid I'd have to fail you. Plagiarism is unforgivable, even if you're only plagiarizing Marlon Brando."

"It expresses what I want to say, though."

"I'm sure it does, but it's not getting us anywhere. Why don't we go to a table, sit down, and talk this over like rational people."

Mason started to say something, but she didn't. She just stood there looking at him, her purse dangling from her right hand.

"Did you ever think about playing softball?" Burns asked her. "You might be pretty good at it."

"What does softball have to do with anything?"

"The college softball team lost its right

fielder yesterday. We need a replacement."

"Well it won't be me. Come on. We'll go have that talk."

She started for her Cadillac. Burns didn't want to ride with her. He'd already been grappled in an elevator. He didn't want to be grappled in a Caddy. He said, "I'll meet you at my car."

Mason was sitting at the picnic table near Burns's Camry when he got there. Her pink car was parked so that he couldn't get his own out on the road again without considerable maneuvering.

"I wasn't going to try to escape," he said.

"I'm the one who was being followed," Mason told him. Her hair was back in place, and she had even done something about her make-up. "So I thought I'd leave myself in the best position to get away. What did you want to talk about?"

Burns sat across from her and rested his arms on the concrete table.

"Neal Bruce," he said.

Chapter 26

It didn't take long for Burns to get the story. Neal Bruce had been married and divorced twice, but he still believed that he had a reputation to guard. After all, Mary Mason explained, he lived in a conservative Texas town and worked in a conservative occupation.

Burns wondered if Boss Napier would have told her that *conservative Texas town* was a redundancy. Probably not, though with Napier you never could tell.

At any rate, Mason told Burns that although she and Bruce were in love and planned to be married, Bruce thought that they should keep their relationship secret until they were ready to make some sort of public announcement.

It didn't make much sense to Burns. Mason and Bruce were both unmarried adults, and they could do whatever they pleased. He didn't see why there would be any objections, and he told Mason as much.

"That shows how much you know. People in this town don't have much to talk about, so when they get hold of something, they make the most of it. Neal and I don't want to be the topic of their discussions."

It was all Burns could do not to say that such considerations had apparently never bothered her before, but somehow he managed to control himself.

Instead he said, "Speaking of people who talk more than they should, did you by any chance pay a condolence call on Mrs. Hart?"

"Of course I did. She's one of my very best Merry Mary customers. I had to go by and tell her how sorry I was about Matt."

"Did she happen to mention toy soldiers to you?"

Mason arched an eyebrow. "Why do you ask?"

"Because of something you said."

"I'm not at all sure what you're talking about."

Burns hadn't wanted to come right out with it, but now he didn't see any other way. "You mentioned that a toy soldier was found by Hart's body. I was wondering how you knew."

"Oh. I see. Well, as a matter of fact, Lonell did say something about that."

"Lonell?"

"That's Mrs. Hart's name, honey."

Honey, Burns thought. He was back in Mason's good graces again. She and Bruce might have an understanding, but that didn't mean she could change her flirtatious ways.

"She shouldn't have said anything about it. Have you told anybody?"

"No. It didn't occur to me to tell anybody."

"Not even Bruce?"

"No. I didn't even think of it again. It didn't seem important."

"Maybe it's not, but I wouldn't mention it if I were you."

"If you say so."

She started to get up, as if she were ready to leave, and Burns reached out and took hold of her wrist.

She sat back down and looked at his hand. She arched the eyebrow again, and Burns quickly let go of her wrist.

"I have something else to ask you," he said, knowing that she wasn't going to like it.

"Why you just go right ahead. I'm beginning to enjoy it here, just you and me with this whole big old park all to ourselves. It's very romantic, don't you think?"

Burns cleared his throat. "It's just a big empty park," he said.

He wished someone else would pay a visit to the place. Why didn't Pecan City's residents take advantage of the amenities provided for them?

"And here we are," Mason said. "Two people, all alone with nothing to do."

Burns vaguely remembered a song with words that echoed those. "True Love?" He wasn't sure, and he didn't want to mention it. What had he been about to ask, anyway? Mason had thrown off his whole train of thought. No matter what people said about her, it was true that she was a very seductive woman.

Not that he was interested. He got his mind back on track and said, "I was wondering about something."

"And I'll bet I know exactly what it is."

He didn't wait for her to tell him what she thought it might be, mainly because he was sure she had an idea completely different from his own. He said, "I have to ask you about why you went to Dr. Partridge and told her that Steven Stilwell was interested in the toy soldiers."

Mason widened her eyes. "But he *is* interested in them. He's an antiques dealer, after all."

"But when I was in Dr. Partridge's office, you made it sound very much like Stilwell was the one who took them from her house. I think you might have been . . . exaggerating."

Burns didn't think it was possible for her eyes to widen any further, but he was wrong.

"Carl, shame on you. You don't think I would tell a lie, do you?"

"I didn't say you lied. I said you might have exaggerated."

"Well, I never!"

"I'm not saying I blame you. For exaggerating, I mean. You were just trying to throw suspicion on someone besides Neal Bruce. You knew he collected soldiers, and you were afraid someone would suspect him of taking the ones that were missing. You were protecting him. I can see that."

Mason's demeanor changed. "I said before that you weren't as nice as you seemed, and now you've tricked me again. First you lure me here to this park and pretend you like being alone with me, and then you accuse me of lying."

Burns was so taken aback that he couldn't answer for a few seconds. After he gathered his thoughts, he said, "I didn't lure you here. I followed you. You're the one who did the luring, if anybody did."

Mason stood up. "Of all things! I never

heard of anything so ridiculous. I don't have to listen to you any more. I've been insulted enough for one day."

"Let me insult you one more time," Burns said.

"I will not. You're impossible."

"This won't insult you. Do you know Rex and Suzanne Cody?"

"Of course I do. I know everybody in Pecan City."

"Do they collect toy soldiers?"

"Why don't you ask them, you little sneak?"

"I'm going to do that as soon as I leave here. But I thought you might be able to help me."

"I don't want to help you. You're just trying to get me in trouble again."

She turned and stalked to her Cadillac, got in, and drove away, spinning the tires so that gravel flew up and clicked against the side of Burns's Camry. He walked over to look for chipped paint, but he didn't detect any.

Mason hadn't admitted a thing, but as far as Burns was concerned, she might as well have. He was convinced that he was right about her lying to protect Bruce. Burns felt that he should have known all along that it was a mistake to believe her. After all, Dr.

Partridge had told him that Mason was capable of anything. However, it was Partridge who had called him and had him listen to Mason's story, so maybe Partridge had thought there was something to it in spite of its source. In the end, it had proved to be just another dead end. Worse than that, it had messed up any case that Burns had been making against Stilwell, who was probably in the clear, an innocent victim not of jealousy but of Mason's being protective of her new lover.

The depressing thing was that Stilwell wasn't the only one in the clear. So was everyone else, unless Napier had found out that Ball had lied about his rifle.

And then there were Rex and Suzanne Cody. Maybe they were the guilty parties. Burns was sure Napier had talked to them, though he hadn't mentioned it. Since they were part of the college family, Burns was sure he was expected to have a chat with them.

He looked at his watch. It was still early afternoon, so he could drive by their house, which, as it happened, wasn't too far from the one owned by the Balls. It could, however, have been on a different planet, for as nice as the Balls' house was, the Codys' was nicer. In fact, *nice* wasn't the word to describe it; neither was *house*. *Mansion* would have been more appropriate, and it was by far the largest home in Pecan City.

Burns decided that he'd pay it a visit.

Chapter 27

Driving through the downtown area, Burns saw that Mason's pink car was parked just down the block from Stilwell's antique store.

Burns thought about the conveniences of living in a small town. Mason could apologize to Stilwell, walk a short distance, and tell Bruce what had happened. You couldn't do that in Houston. Well, you could, but it would be unlikely that the buildings would be so close together. And Burns was willing to bet there weren't a lot of antique stores in downtown Houston.

He stopped at the college and went up to his office to tell Bunni where he was going and to ask if he'd had any calls or visitors.

Bunni told him that, as usual, there had been none of either.

"I won't be back this afternoon," he said. "If anyone calls, just take a message."

Bunni said she would and asked if the baseball game was still on for Saturday.

Burns hadn't thought about it, but with the injury to Elliott, the faculty team wasn't at full strength. And it might not be safe to play, what with someone sitting around waiting to pick off members of the team. Even if Napier had the metal building guarded, there was always a chance something could happen.

"I'm not sure," Burns said. "Maybe not."

He didn't add that he sincerely hoped not. He wouldn't have to humiliate himself in front of Elaine and everybody else.

"I'll find out," he said, feeling better about things for the first time all day.

The Cody house, or mansion, sat at the top of Thrill Hill and looked down on all the other lesser homes around. It was surrounded by a high wrought-iron fence. A sign attached to the fence said "The Cody's" in old English script, and Burns reflected on the sad fact that even having millions of dollars didn't protect people from the egregious misuse of the apostrophe.

There was an electronically operated gate beside the sign, but it was open, so Burns drove through it and onto the grounds. The drive was paved, and it curved around in front of the house so that Burns was able to park almost at the door. He was prevented from getting really close by the wide concrete porch and the steps that led up to it.

The house was a wonderful example of

conspicuous consumption. It was modeled on the antebellum mansions of Mississippi, and Burns almost expected to see someone sitting on the veranda, wearing a white suit and a planter's hat, sipping on a mint julep. At the very least he expected the doorbell to play "Dixie."

If it did, he couldn't hear it. The house was too well insulated for that.

Or maybe the bell didn't work, because no one came to the door in response to it. Burns pushed it again and waited. Still no one came. Burns was a little surprised. He'd more or less expected a liveried servant to appear. The Codys were a little too democratic for that, he supposed.

Because of the open gate, Burns knew that the Codys must be at home. Maybe he should have known the people of his station entered a place like this only through the back door. He walked down off the porch and started around the house on a little graveled path that wound among the trees on the close-clipped lawn. When he got near the back, he could hear the sounds of people talking, and he soon saw that the Codys were enjoying the pleasant weather in their back yard on their own private putting green. Burns looked around, and he was disappointed that there were no mint juleps anywhere to be seen.

"Excuse me," he said.

Rex Cody, who had been lining up a putt, straightened and turned around. Suzanne looked at him with curiosity, as if he might have wandered in from the slave quarters in some trashy plantation novel. If Burns had been wearing a hat, he would have taken it off and twisted it in his hands.

"I hate to bother you," Burns began, but Cody interrupted him.

"Whatever you're selling, we don't want any."

"I told you we should have that gate fixed," Suzanne said.

She was in her late thirties, Burns thought, and she looked trim and fit in the white shorts and shirt she was wearing. Her husband was a little older and not as fit. His stomach pushed out his polo shirt and obscured the waistband of his golfing shorts.

"I'm not selling anything," Burns told them, and Cody interrupted again.

"That's what they all say, buddy. Now get on your horse and ride on out of here."

"Actually I'm in a Toyota."

The Codys exchanged glances, as if to say, "How plebeian. And a smart-ass, besides."

"I teach at the college," Burns continued.

"My name's Carl Burns, and I'm the chair of the English Department. Dean Partridge asked me to come by and visit with you."

"Oh," Suzanne said. "Then we beg your pardon. We didn't know you were here on college business. I've contributed quite a bit of money to the school, as I'm sure you must know."

"Oh, yes," Burns said, wondering if he should curtsy. "The college is very indebted to you for the furnishings in the student center, among other things."

Suzanne smiled, and Burns could see that she appreciated the acknowledgment.

"Why don't we sit down," she said, leading the way to a white metal table shaded by a large cloth umbrella, also white.

Rex looked reluctantly at the golf ball at his feet. He sighed, flipped the club, caught it by the handle, and followed his wife. Burns trailed along behind.

When they were seated at the table, Rex said, "Make it snappy, Dr. Burns. It is *doctor*, I presume."

"It is, but just call me Carl."

"Fine. You know who we are, and we know you. Now that we're all cozy, state your business and let's get this over with."

Burns wondered if Cody dealt with everyone the same way, or if he treated only those he regarded as his underlings with disdain.

"I'm here because someone stole some toy soldiers from Dr. Partridge's house," Burns said.

"Jesus Christ," Rex said. "And you interrupted my putting practice for that?"

"She thinks you might have stolen them," Burns told him.

He didn't know why he said it. It was uncharacteristic of him. He decided that he'd been hanging around Napier for too long.

"The nerve of that woman," Suzanne said. "We'll just see how long it takes us to get her ass fired."

Burns couldn't hide his smile. "Did you say *ass?*"

"What the hell difference does it make?" Rex said. "She can say whatever she damn well pleases. I'm not going to have anybody call me a thief and send some second-rate English teacher to my own house to question me."

The golf club was leaning against the table, and Burns wondered what would happen if he took it and bent it over Cody's head. Probably he'd be thrown in the Pecan City jail, where Boss Napier would work him over with the bullwhip.

"If we're going by the salary that I'm paid,

I'm more like a third-rate English teacher," Burns said.

"Whatever you're getting, it's more than you deserve."

Things had gone bad fast, Burns thought. Maybe it was just a case of instant mutual dislike, or maybe Cody was guilty of something. Whatever the case, Burns wasn't going to find out anything at this rate. Time to change tactics and get back to being the real Carl Burns instead of some disrespectful imposter.

"I'm sorry if I've offended you," he said, trying to sound contrite. "I seem to have implied something that's not true, and I don't blame you for being upset."

"Upset?" Rex said. "Am I upset? Do I look upset, Suzie?"

He looked like a man about to have an apoplexy, Burns thought, but Suzanne said, "Not at all, Rex. You look very calm to me."

If that was true, Burns didn't want to see him when he was actually upset.

"At any rate," Burns said. "I've gotten off on the wrong foot with you. When I told you that Dr. Partridge thinks you might have stolen her soldiers, I was exaggerating. I should have said that you and your wife were among the few people who were in her house on the day they disappeared. Dr. Partridge hoped that you might have seen or heard something that would help us find out who took them."

"It sure didn't sound that way to me," Rex said, and Suzanne said, "Me neither."

"I didn't mean to offend you. I'm sorry about that."

"You damn well should be. I've a good mind to have *your* ass fired."

He could do it, too, but at the moment Burns didn't even care. He was just sorry he'd ever let Partridge talk him into this. Partridge and Napier. It was all their fault.

"You're pretty defensive," he said, feeling the imposter slipping out again. "Is it because you're guilty?"

"Hell no, I'm not guilty. If I wanted any toy soldiers, I'd buy them myself." Rex waved a hand to indicate his house and grounds. "Do I look like someone who needs to steal some crummy toy soldiers?"

"No," Burns said. "You certainly don't."

"And I didn't, either." Rex stood up. "So you can leave now."

Burns sat right where he was. "I have another question for you."

Rex picked up his golf club and ran his left hand down the shaft.

"I'm wondering if you or Mrs. Cody saw anybody else with an undue interest in the soldiers. Anybody who might have lingered in the room to be alone with them."

"There was no chance of that," Suzanne said.

Rex continued to finger the shaft of his golf club. Burns wondered if Rex knew the Freudian implications of that action. Probably not.

"There were students there," Suzanne said. "Bustling around, telling us that we'd come in the wrong way, showing us out. We weren't in there long enough to have taken anything, and neither was anyone else."

"What about Matthew Hart?" Burns asked. "How well did you know him?"

"What the hell does he have to do with anything?" Rex said.

"I was just wondering."

"Hart was a bastard," Rex said. "But that doesn't mean I didn't like him. We played bridge with him and his wife now and then. You, on the other hand, I don't like much at all."

"I'm not much of a bridge player," Burns said.

"Probably not much of anything. Now why don't you take a hike."

Burns didn't think he was going to get anything more out of the Codys. He stood up and said, "Thanks for taking the time to talk to me."

"You shouldn't barge in on people," Rex said, fondling the club. "They don't like it."

"I apologize," Burns said. "But when the dean speaks, I obey."

"Maybe you're not all bad, then," Rex said, but Burns could tell he didn't really mean it.

Chapter 28

As Burns drove around the curving drive, he reflected that he could see most of Pecan City from the Codys' lot. It wasn't a bad little town, he thought. He could see the college, the Main Building standing out from the others by virtue of being the only one with more than two stories. He could also see the downtown area and Neal Bruce's bank, which stood out for the same reason Main did. Burns wondered if Bruce and Mason would ever really get married or if Bruce was just another in a long line of her conquests.

Looking in the direction of the baseball field, Burns noted that he could see it quite well, and the metal building where the shooter had been positioned sparkled in the sun. It wouldn't have been all that tricky for Cody to fire the shot that hit Don Elliott and then get back home, if he had the stamina to walk up Thrill Hill. He looked in rotten shape to Burns, who thought climbing the stairs in Main had conditioned him enough so that he could get up the hill on foot if he'd wanted to try it, which he didn't. Better to think that he could do it than to be disillusioned by the reality.

Thrill Hill, which was quite steep, had been named by high school students of generations long past. When there had been nothing more than a dirt road to the top, they had driven up there in their jalopies, turned around, and driven back down as fast as they could go. When the road leveled out at the bottom, it ran straight for a quarter of a mile after its junction with the main road, so there was plenty of time to slow down, assuming there was no one coming along to get in the way and prevent the crossing.

As he pulled out of the Codys' drive, Burns wondered if Rex Cody had always been an asshole or if he'd become one only after he got rich in the oil business. Burns remembered what F. Scott Fitzgerald had said about the very rich: "They are different from you and me." Hemingway hadn't thought much of that idea. He believed the only difference was that the rich had more money. Burns wasn't sure who was right, but Rex Cody was different from Burns, and if it was money that had made him that way, Burns wanted no part of it.

But, Burns told himself, he'd never become like Cody. If he had money, he'd be kind and generous and beloved by the community. He'd use his wealth for the benefit of all. No question about it.

Burns stared down the hill, his head filled with all the wonderful things he would do, not to mention all the civic awards he'd receive, so that at first he didn't notice the car that was coming up the hill. When he did notice, he saw that it was coming straight for him.

The road was paved, and there was plenty of room for both cars. But the driver of the car headed up was taking his half of the road right out of the middle.

The sun dazzled off the car's windshield, and Burns couldn't see who was driving or whether he was even looking in Burns's direction.

Probably some jerk talking on a cell phone, Burns thought, and honked the Camry's horn. The result was disappointing. Say what you might about the old gas-guzzler that Burns's ancient Plymouth had been, it had a real horn on it. It had honked with *gravitas* and authority. It had moved people out of the way with its stentorian tones.

The horn on the Camry didn't have anything like the same resonance or force, and it sounded to Burns about as authoritative as the little squeeze-bulb horn that had been on the Huffy bike he'd gotten when he was five years old.

If the driver in the other car heard it at all, he gave no sign. The voice on his cell phone was no doubt louder than the horn.

Burns glanced to his right for some way to escape. There was really no place for him to go. There were no houses on the hill other than the Cody mansion, so there were no driveways or yards that offered a convenient turn-in. There was just a slight drop-off onto the rough and rocky shoulder in which only a few weeds grew, and the shoulder itself was narrow, no more than a couple of feet wide. A drainage ditch ran along beside it, and beyond that some scrawny mesquite bushes and a few runty oaks stuck up behind the barbed wire fence that went all the way down the hill.

Even worse, right ahead there was a culvert underneath the road, and on each side of the road there was a large concrete abutment. Burns had literally nowhere to turn.

Burns slowed down. The other driver didn't, and he seemed to have no intention of moving out of the middle of the road.

As a teenager, Burns had heard about the game of *chicken*. He hadn't thought about it in years, however, and he'd certainly never taken part in it.

Well, he thought, he hadn't taken part in it then, but he was taking part in it now, and it didn't take him long to decide that when it came to being chicken, he had few peers. Better to try to miss the abutment than to hit the other car head on. As the driver barreled closer, Burns threw on the brakes and turned off the road.

The Camry dropped off the pavement and slid toward the abutment. Burns hoped he could stop before he hit it. The anti-lock brakes helped, but Burns still found himself in a skid that he couldn't control, heading straight for tons of solid concrete.

Burns wrenched the steering wheel, and he could almost feel the tires turning underneath the Camry. But there was no traction on the loose soil and rocks. The car was still going straight.

Bootlegger's turn, Burns thought, having heard the term somewhere or read it in a book. He stepped on the emergency brake.

That worked, if you could call it working. The car turned sharply sideways, and now the side instead of the hood was headed for the abutment.

Burns reached down, smacking his head on the wheel, and released the parking brake, mashing the accelerator at the same time. Somehow the back tires grabbed hold, and the Camry shot past the abutment with about an inch to spare. Burns didn't know how close he actually was because he had closed his eyes.

The car bottomed out in the ditch, and Burns bounced straight up. His eyes came open as the Camry slid up the side of the ditch and into the barbed wire strands of the fence. The wires twanged apart, but Burns didn't hear the music they made as the car rocked from side to side and tried to flip itself over.

It stayed upright, slid past a mesquite bush whose thorns screeched down its side, and came to a stop in front of a scraggly oak.

For several seconds Burns did nothing more than sit there and breathe. The car's engine was still running, and the air-conditioner was pumping cool air, but Burns was sweating. After a while he managed to pry his fingers loose from the steering wheel and assess the damage to himself.

There was none, as far as he could tell, glad for once that he always buckled his seat belt. He unbuckled it with shaking fingers and got out of the car, finding that his legs would hold him up just fine even though his knees were a bit watery.

There were long scratches down the side of the Camry, and the barbed wire had scored the hood, but there didn't seem to be any other damage. Burns had insurance, and he could have the car repainted, but it wouldn't seem new anymore.

He looked up the hill, but of course there was no sign of the car that had forced him off the road. He hadn't expected that there would be. The road went on past the Codys' house and along the crest of the hill before it curved around and down toward a little town named Butler, about ten miles away. Along the way to Butler, there were plenty of little county roads that a driver could take if he wanted to return to Pecan City. Burns figured the driver who had forced him off the road was cruising happily along one of them, jabbering away on his cell phone about the mesquite bushes, or maybe only asking for directions.

Burns wiped sweat off his forehead and turned to have a look at the path he had taken from the road. He supposed he could turn around and drive back that way. Might as well give it a try.

Navigating the ditch wasn't any fun, even driving very slowly, but Burns managed it without incident and got back onto the road. The car seemed to be running just fine, and there weren't even any new rattles.

Burns thought for a second about going

up the hill to let Cody know that his fence was down, but Cody would probably want Burns to pay for the damage. Burns wasn't in any mood for that, and since he hadn't seen any cattle that might wander out onto the road, he didn't think there was any danger to drivers, not that there was any traffic to speak of. He decided to wait until he got back to town and make an anonymous call from a pay phone at some convenience store.

Burns turned on the radio, hoping to find some soothing music. He turned to the country station, where Kerry Newcomb was singing his latest hit, something about a ramblin' man named Poudre River Pete and his "amorous, three-legged, beer-swilling cur."

Not exactly soothing, Burns thought as he punched a button. He got a news story about another soldier dying in a riot in Iraq, which was even less soothing, so he punched another button, this one for an oldies station out of Dallas. Buddy Holly was doing "Words of Love," which was just right, and Burns was momentarily soothed.

Then he thought about what Boss Napier would say when he told him about the near-miss on Thrill Hill.

"Details, Burns. Didn't we talk about

that? You have to get the details. What was the make of car? How about the year? Or the color? What was the license number?"

Burns couldn't answer any of those questions, but then he'd been more intent on getting off the road in one piece than in taking an inventory of the approaching car's vital statistics.

"Thinking of yourself," Napier would say, his lip curling with contempt. "That's an English teacher for you. How do you expect me to make an arrest if you don't have any of the necessary details?"

And so on.

It was too horrible to contemplate, so Burns figured he just wouldn't mention it. After all, there were plenty of bad drivers in Pecan City, and he'd encountered one of them in an awkward spot. That's all there was to it. Except that try as he might, Burns couldn't convince himself of that. Even his cell phone theory seemed to him a flimsy construction now. There had been something deliberate in the way the car headed for him and didn't waver, though Burns couldn't think of any reason why someone would want to hurt him.

Of course he couldn't think of any reason why anyone would want to hurt Matthew Hart, Mal Tomlin, and Don Elliott, either.

Or why anyone would want to steal Dr. Partridge's toy soldiers. Maybe Boss Napier had come up with something, but for the moment Burns preferred to forget the whole thing and go home, which is what he did.

Chapter 29

There was a message on Burns's answering machine from Mal Tomlin.

"In case you were wondering," Mal's voice said, "the game is still on for Saturday."

Damn, Burns thought.

"If we don't play," Mal went on, "the terrorists win."

Burns wasn't sure of many things, but he was absolutely convinced that terrorists had nothing at all to do with the shootings.

"I know what you're thinking," Mal said, "but it's the same thing. The students will think we're gutless if we're afraid to go out there."

But we don't have a right fielder, Burns thought.

"Walt Melling says he'll try to play right field," Mal continued. "He won't cover much ground, but nobody ever hits the ball to right field. We'll be fine."

Not if the sniper strikes again, Burns thought.

"I called Boss Napier," Mal said, "and he

agrees that the game should go on. There'll be a big police presence, and he's sure there won't be any shooting."

Dandy, Burns thought. *So I'll get to humiliate myself after all.*

"I know you'll do great things," Mal said. "That home run you hit was something else. Do it again, and you'll be a hero."

Fat chance, Burns thought, and Mal didn't have an answer for that one.

"I'll see you at practice," Mal's message continued.

What about the sniper? Burns wondered.

"In case you're worried," Mal said, "the cops will be there this afternoon, too. According to your pal Napier, they've been all over the neighborhood for most of the day, looking for tips on the sniper. So we'll be well protected."

Dandy, Burns thought.

"Wear your hitting shoes."

Like I own a pair, Burns thought. He wished that Mal were standing there so he could light into him. But Mal wasn't there, and the message was over, so Burns got dressed and went to the practice field.

Boss Napier was sitting in the stands when Burns arrived. Burns stood at the entrance to the dugout and pretended not to see him.

The grass had been cut that day, and Burns liked the smell. He liked the way the grass looked, green and level. He hated mowing, but he liked the results.

Mal Tomlin was hitting flies for the outfielders. The sound of the fat part of the bat hitting the ball was another thing that Burns liked. He wouldn't mind standing there all afternoon, ignoring Napier, smelling the grass, and listening to the bat smack the ball.

"Hey, Burns," Napier called from the stands, "come here a second."

Burns looked out at the field. Mal Tomlin wasn't paying any attention to him, so he figured he had a few minutes to spare, and he was going to have to face Napier sooner or later. He climbed up the stands, tossed down his glove, and sat by the police chief.

"Going to hit another home run today?" Napier said when Burns had settled himself.

Burns looked out over the field. Mal hit a long fly to Walt Melling in right. Walt wasn't exactly a gazelle, but he managed to get under the ball and catch it. He threw it back in to Abner Swan. It bounced three times and then rolled the rest of the way. Swan picked it up and tossed it to Mal, who hit another fly.

"I didn't hit a home run," Burns said, not

looking at Napier. "Somebody tagged me out."

"Look, Burns," Napier said, "I didn't mean to rain on your parade. If you want to call it a home run, go ahead and call it a home run."

"It was only practice. It didn't really count anyway."

"I never realized how good you were at feeling sorry for yourself. You have a real talent for it."

"I'm an English teacher. We're very self-absorbed."

"Yeah, I can believe it." Napier pointed out over the field and toward Thrill Hill, where Burns could not quite make out the Cody mansion among the trees. "Ever been up there?"

Burns wondered, not for the first time, if Napier didn't know a lot more about what was going on in Pecan City than Burns realized. And then he remembered that he'd neglected to call Cody about that broken fence. There might well be a connection between Napier's question and that broken fence, but Burns wasn't going to ask about it.

"I've been there," he said.

"Today?"

Burns turned slightly and looked at

Napier. "Why do I get the feeling you already know the answer to that?"

"Because you think I'm omnipotent?"

Burns couldn't help staring.

Napier got a smug look. "I'll bet you didn't think I knew words like that, did you, Burns? Well, I do. I'm not a complete jerk, after all."

"You always act like a jerk when *I* use a word like that."

"That's because you're an English teacher, and you're showing off to prove you're smarter than everybody else."

"I am not. And even if I were, how does that make what you were doing any different?"

"The difference is that I was showing off to prove I'm not a complete jerk. Anyway, I'm not really omnipotent. It's just that I got a complaint from Rex Cody about a certain Dr. Carl Burns who showed up at his place, asked all kinds of questions, and then drove through his fence."

Burns wondered how Cody knew who'd wrecked the fence. "He can't prove a thing."

Napier turned around and stretched his neck to look at the parking lot where Burns's Camry sat. After giving the Camry a long look, he turned back to Burns and said,

"I wouldn't be so sure of that."

"All right, ya dirty copper, but you'll never take me alive."

Burns stood up and jogged to the top of the stands, which wasn't far, as there were only ten rows of seats. When he got to the last one, he turned around and raised his arms to the sky.

"Top of the world, Ma!" he yelled.

Napier just sat where he was, shaking his head and not looking in Burns's direction. However, several of the faculty team members stopped what they were doing on the field and looked at him as if he had gone crazy.

Burns stared back at them and held his pose for a couple of seconds. Then he shrugged, walked back down, and sat beside Napier again.

"You do a lousy Cagney," Napier said.

"You dirty rat," Burns said. "You killed my brother, you dirty rat."

"That was even worse. I'll give you a tip, Burns. Give up show business and stick to teaching kids about Edgar Allan Poe."

"I'll think about it."

"Good. Did you find out anything from Cody?"

"Just that I don't like him much. He didn't confess to shooting anybody, and I can't really see why he would. I can see why somebody might want to shoot him, though."

"Why did you drive through his fence?"

Burns would have preferred not to discuss it, but Napier wasn't the type to let the subject drop. So Burns told him the whole story.

"Those cell phones are a menace, all right," Napier said when Burns was finished. "If you're sure that's what it was. What kind of car was the guy driving?"

"I knew you were going to ask me that," Burns said, and he went on to tell Napier all the things he didn't know.

"You're a big help, Burns. You and that Poe are about on a par when it comes to the details."

"I knew you were going to say that, too, so you can spare me the rest of the lecture. Why don't you just tell me what you found out today."

"You nearly get killed, and you want me to tell you what I found out today? I think we should talk about the accident, if that's what it was."

"I don't want to talk about the accident. That's all it was, and there's no point in trying to make anything else out of it."

"If you say so. But don't you think it's a

285

little suspicious that you were nearly killed in the course of an investigation that you're involved in?"

"I'm not involved in an investigation. I'm just asking questions because you and Dr. Partridge wanted me to do it. Nobody knew where I was. So there's no way anybody could have tried to run me off the road."

"All right. I believe you."

Burns listened to Mal, who was encouraging Walt Melling to show a little more hustle. The players on the field were no longer paying any attention to Burns and Napier.

"I'm glad you believe me," Burns said. "Now, I've showed you mine. You show me yours."

Napier said that he'd had a call from Harvey Ball, who'd given him the name of the place where he'd sent his rifle for repair.

"And sure enough, they told you they have it," Burns said. "What a shock. As if they'd say anything else after Ball called them."

"They told me they had it for repair," Napier said. "And I believe them. It's not the kind of place that would lie for a customer. It's too big for that."

"Did anybody in the Balls' neighborhood see the sniper yesterday?"

"Not that we've found out so far, and we've talked to just about all of them. But you know how it is. People are inside, watching TV, or in their back yards. Nobody's watching for some strange car on the street."

"What if he parked near the building where the shots were fired?"

"Now that's a good question, Burns. We went over that area pretty well yesterday, and we don't think that's what happened. We think he got away through the neighborhood. So someone may have seen him. We'll keep looking."

Burns shrugged. He didn't think Napier would find anything. People were too unobservant.

"What about Bruce?" Napier asked. "He have anything to tell you?"

"Probably nothing an omnipotent cop like you doesn't know already."

"You'd better tell me anyway. Sometimes I'm not as omnipotent as I am at others."

Burns told him about his talk with Bruce and about what had happened with Mary Mason afterward.

"You're always getting beaten up by women," Napier said. "You should stay away from them."

"She didn't beat me up. She just hit me with her purse."

"Sounds like she rattled you around pretty good, if you ask me."

"I don't recall asking. Anyway, the important thing is that she tried to frame Stilwell for the theft of the soldiers because she and Bruce are an item. So that lets Stilwell off the hook."

"Nobody's ever off the hook, Burns."

"I think Stilwell is. I've hit a wall on this whole thing. I'm not doing you any good, my car's a mess, and I'm making a lot of people very angry. Some of that anger's going to transfer to the college, and Dr. Partridge is going to be upset with me."

"What are you trying to tell me, Burns? You don't have to weasel around with me. Don't you tell your students to get to the point without being weasels?"

Burns admitted that he did, though not using that exact terminology.

"I thought so. Well, it doesn't matter. I know what you're saying. You're saying you want to quit, but you can't get out of it now. For all we know, you might be a target yourself. That little 'accident' of yours should have proved that to you."

"Different M.O.," Burns said. "Isn't that what you cops say?"

"Very good, Burns. You have cop lingo down pat. You must've watched *Dragnet* once upon a time."

"True. That new version, though, that one sucks."

"The theme song's not bad," Napier said. "Aside from that, it's just another cop show."

"True. Did you visit Don Elliott in the hospital today?"

"Yeah. He couldn't think of anybody who'd shoot him. That's your job, Burns. You're supposed to figure stuff like that out, solve the crime, and make me look good."

"It never happened that way on *Dragnet*. Joe Friday didn't need any help."

"He wasn't dealing with a bunch of nutty college teachers, either, was he?"

"I guess not," Burns said. "But if he had been, he and Frank would have solved the case on their own."

"That's why we have TV," Napier said. "To make things work out the way they should. This isn't like that. Have you talked to Elliott?"

"No, and I don't think I will."

"You could go by after practice."

Burns was going to say that he didn't think he would, but he didn't get the chance.

"Burns!" Mal Tomlin yelled from the field. "Get on down here. It's time for some infield practice."

Burns had been dreading this moment. He was tired of talking to Napier, but he didn't want to have to go out on the field. He knew he wasn't a good ballplayer, and he was going to be embarrassed enough on Saturday. He didn't want to have Napier watching him now.

"Don't you have some sleuthing to do?" Burns said.

"Nope," Napier said. "I'm going to watch you practice. See how you turn the double play."

Burns stood up and waited to see if Napier would make any hernia jokes. He didn't, which was a mark in his favor.

"I don't do the turn very well," Burns said, bending down to pick up his glove. "But sometimes I can do it without falling down."

"I'm looking forward to seeing that," Napier said.

Burns slipped his hand into his glove and pounded his fist into the pocket a couple of times.

"I'll bet you are," he said.

Chapter 30

To his surprise, Burns didn't do too badly during the infield practice. None of Dorinda Edgely's throws from third hit him in the face when they tried an around-the-horn double play, he didn't trip over his own feet, and he didn't throw the ball into the dugout when he was trying to get it to the first baseman. No one would ever mistake him for a natural athlete, but at least he held his own with the other amateurs.

Then Tomlin said it was time for a little batting practice. Burns let everyone go in front of him, hoping that Napier would get bored and leave. He should have known better. When Burns stood in the batting box, the police chief was still in the stands, watching.

Burns wondered what the odds were that he would hit another ball over the fence. Probably about the same as winning Lotto Texas. He didn't know what those odds were, but he calculated that there was as much likelihood of winning as there was of getting eaten by a great white shark in

Odessa, Texas, during a sandstorm.

Mal was pitching batting practice because he didn't want to take any chances with Dawn Melling's arm on the day before the big game.

"Those students won't show us any mercy," Mal said from the mound. "They'll pitch you inside, and they might even hit you. It would give them a chance to get back at you for those bad grades."

There were some uneasy laughs, and Abner Swan stepped into the batter's box to take a few swings. He was wearing overalls again, and he looked like a farmer on a trip to buy some chicken feed. He waggled the bat around a couple of times, and when he settled into his stance, he seemed awkward and uneasy. But he hit the ball squarely several times.

"Those would be hits in any league," Mal said. "Way to go, Abner."

Burns wasn't interested in watching the others hit. They could all hit better than he could, with the possible exception of Walt Melling. Burns hadn't seen him at bat and had no idea about his ability.

Thinking about what Mal had said about students and bad grades, Burns wondered again if an irate student could be behind the shootings, but he knew that couldn't be it.

Hart hadn't taught at the college for years, and Burns still didn't believe a student would try to get revenge for some old hurt that should have healed long ago.

Dorinda Edgely took Abner's place in the box. She looked compact and confident, and she hit the first ball over Walt Melling's head. It went all the way to the fence. She grinned, swished the bat over the plate a few times, and hit Tomlin's next pitch in the same place. Burns had never hit two balls in a row that well in his entire life.

After a few more solid knocks, Dorinda jogged out to take Walt's place.

"You go ahead," Burns said when Walt reached the plate. "I don't mind waiting."

"You sure?"

"I'm sure," Burns said, glancing around to see if Napier had left yet.

He hadn't, so Burns picked up a bat and tried to pretend he knew what to do with it as Walt stepped into the box. He thought about all that he'd gone through that day, none of which would contribute anything toward making him a better hitter. And none of which would contribute anything to the solving of the case.

Or would it? Something was niggling at the back of Burns's mind, and it seemed to him that there might be a clue that he'd missed, some crucial detail that he hadn't mentioned even to Napier.

Walt Melling turned out to be a natural hitter. He had a smooth, deceptively easy swing and good bat speed. He knocked one pitch over the fence in left and one deep into center field.

"Things are looking up," Mal said. "I miss Don, but all he could do was work the pitcher for walks. You're going to get some runs for us, Walt."

At another time, Burns might have envied Melling's prowess, but as his turn came to bat, he was too absorbed in his thoughts about the shootings to concentrate. He missed the first pitch by at least a foot. He missed the second one even more.

"You're swinging like a rusty gate," Tomlin said. "Hit one like you did yesterday."

Instead, Burns hit a vicious foul that sailed back and slapped into the fence right in front of the stands where Napier was sitting.

"You'll have to do better than that," Tomlin said, but Burns still didn't have his mind on hitting. Which might have explained why he knocked the next pitch over the right field fence, almost in the same spot where he'd hit one the day before. If he'd been thinking about it, he'd never have been able to do it.

"Way to go!" Tomlin yelled, obviously surprised. "We're going to make a hitter out of you yet."

Burns hardly realized what he'd done at first, but when it finally dawned on him, he looked around for Napier. All he saw was the police chief's car as it pulled out of the lot. Napier had left too soon to see the home run. That was fine with Burns. It was only practice, and it didn't count anyway. But at least this time no one was going to tag him out.

After the practice, Mal told everyone when to meet the next day for the game.

"Some of you might be going to Hart's funeral," he said, "but that's in the morning. There's nothing disrespectful about carrying on with the game at five o'clock. Matthew would want it that way."

Burns didn't think that Mal had a clue as to what Hart would have wanted, but a little thing like that never bothered Mal.

"You should all be here by four for a little batting and fielding practice," Mal said. "We want the students to know we're just as full of energy as they are."

Burns didn't feel full of energy. He felt tired and worn out. He started toward his

Camry, his mind still occupied with all the things that had crowded into it over the course of the last three days. As a person who liked to make lists, he thought he should sit down and make one. Maybe it would clear up some of the things that were worrying him.

Mal caught up with him in the parking lot and asked if he was all right.

"You look like you've been run over by a bus," Mal said.

Burns assured him that he was fine. "Just tired. How about you?"

"A little worried," Mal said. "I don't like the idea of everybody being out here in the open tomorrow. What if the sniper strikes again?"

"The sniper strikes again," Burns said. "Sounds like an episode of *The Shadow*."

Mal frowned. "This isn't a joke, like some old radio program."

"*The Shadow*'s no joke. We could all learn something from Lamont Cranston. Besides, you said there was going to be plenty of police protection tomorrow, so we don't have a thing to worry about."

"Yeah, you're probably right. Anyway, just keep hitting the ball like you have been, and you'll be the star of the game."

"I don't want to be the star. I just don't

want to disgrace myself."

"You're worried about what Elaine will think, huh?"

Burns started to deny it and then figured that he might as well not bother. Mal would never believe him.

"Don't worry," Mal said. "You'll be fine."

"That's easy for you to say," Burns told him.

They laughed at that, and Mal went to his car. Burns got in his Camry and dug a pen and a piece of paper out of the console. He never liked to be far from writing materials. He sat in the fading light and started making his list.

When he was finished, he read it over. Twice. Then he opened the console and got out his cell phone. As a general rule, Burns wasn't fond of cell phones. He saw, and heard, other people using them all the time, in drive-through lines at the bank or the Whopper Burger, in the halls of the college buildings, on the streets, on the college grounds, in the post office. Everywhere.

Burns wondered what all those people had to say that was so important that it couldn't wait. Maybe that was because he never had anything that important to say.

However, in spite of his antipathy to the

constant cellular chatter, Burns did own a cell phone. Most of the time he kept it in the console of his car. He liked the idea of having it there in case of some dire emergency. Or in case he wanted to call someone about dropping by for a visit, which is what he did now.

Dean Partridge answered on the first ring and said it would be all right for Burns to stop by her house on his way home.

He asked if Billy was on the loose. He didn't want to risk another encounter with her goat. The first one had been more than enough.

"I'll be sure he doesn't pose a threat to you," said Dr. Partridge, and Burns thought she was suppressing a laugh.

Let her laugh, he thought. To her the goat was an animal companion and a method of lawn maintenance. To him it was a public menace.

"I'll be there in about an hour," Burns said, hoping that would give her time to tie the goat securely. "I have a couple of stops to make first."

"Is this important?" Partridge asked.

"I think so," he told her. "I'll know more by the time I get there."

Burns went by the college first. Main was

locked because it was after five o'clock, and there were no classes on Friday night. Burns had to use his key to get in.

He stopped at the soft drink machine at the foot of the stairs to buy a Pepsi One. There was a hand-printed note taped to the plastic front of the machine. It said:

DO NOT!!
PUT CANS IN TRASH!!!
PUT IN RECYCLE BARRELL!!!
MAID ROSE

Rose was the housekeeper in charge of Main, and she was offended by the slovenly habits of most of the people who inhabited it. Lately she had taken special offense at people who casually tossed their empty soft-drink cans into the trash rather than into one of the convenient recycle barrels that were located in the building. She never said anything to anyone directly. Her method was to leave notes for everyone to see. She was weak on spelling, but strong on exclamation marks.

Burns told himself that he would be careful about where he deposited his drink can and went on up the stairs that creaked under his weight. It wasn't that he was heavy. It was just that the building was old, and even when it was deserted, it creaked and groaned like a very old man getting out of bed in the morning.

Burns let himself into his office, and as he opened the door, he heard a lizard scuttle through the ivy outside one of the windows. Overhead in the attic, a pigeon cooed. There had once been a campaign to eliminate the pigeons, but it hadn't worked out. Burns just hoped his ceiling didn't collapse from the accumulated weight of the pigeon droppings above him, or, if it did, that he wouldn't be there when it happened.

He turned on the computer and drank some of his Pepsi while he waited for it to get itself ready for him. When the programs were all loaded, he went back into the student files that he had looked at previously. This time he was searching for information on a particular person. Having practiced with the system only the evening before, he found what he was looking for fairly quickly. He jotted the information down on a piece of paper and stuck it in his pocket. Then he drank some more Pepsi and thought about things.

There was a Pecan City phone book on the shelf by his desk, and he took it down to look up Matthew Hart's number. When he found it, he punched it on the phone and got Mrs. Hart. After he explained who he was, he asked if he could come by to offer his sympathies.

"Were you a friend of Matthew's?" she asked.

"I teach at the college," Burns said, which was the truth if it wasn't an answer to the question.

It satisfied Mrs. Hart, however, and she told him that he would be welcome.

He locked his office and went downstairs to his car, making sure to put the Pepsi can in a recycle barrel on the way.

Burns might cross Dean Partridge.

He might even cross the president.

But he knew better than to cross Rose.

Chapter 31

The Harts' house, while not a mansion, was very nice indeed, much newer than Burns's own home. The landscaping looked as if it might have been done by a professional, and the lawn was neatly trimmed. Burns was sure the place was well insured.

He parked at the curb and glanced across the street at the vacant lots. There were trees there, and some brush. A sniper could easily have concealed himself and gotten away without being seen. Burns didn't think anyone was there now, however.

Mrs. Hart came to the door in answer to Burns's ring. He was painfully conscious that he wasn't dressed for a condolence call. In his shorts and T-shirt, he looked as if he'd just finished mowing a lawn, but Mrs. Hart didn't seem to notice.

She was a small woman with a lined face and gray hair, and she wore a black dress that looked new. Burns thought she must have bought it for the funeral. He introduced himself, and she invited him in and led him to a small living room, where she sat rigidly in a wooden rocker and he sat on a couch with cushions that offered very little support.

"Did you teach with Matthew?" she asked.

"I came to the college after he retired," Burns said. "But I heard a lot about him from the other instructors."

He didn't mention that most of what he'd heard was bad. There was no need to go into that.

"He was well thought of by everyone," Mrs. Hart said, as if she were oblivious to her husband's reputation. "I know they all hated for him to retire."

Burns didn't disillusion her. He let her reminisce about her husband's teaching career for awhile, and then led the subject around to the one he was interested in.

"You have to wonder why anyone would want to hurt him," Burns said. "And to leave that silly toy soldier lying by him."

Mrs. Hart frowned. "How did you know about the soldier? The police asked me not to mention that to anyone."

"I think Mary Mason told me. Aren't you the one who told her?"

Mrs. Hart sat with her hands folded in her lap. She didn't rock in the chair. She hardly moved. "I must have. A lot of people don't like Mary, but she's always been very nice to me."

No wonder, Burns thought uncharitably. *She fooled around with your husband, so she covered that by playing up to you.*

"She was one of the first to come by after Matthew . . . died," Mrs. Hart continued. "We've known her for years. I buy all my Merry Mary products from her, and she called as soon as she heard the news. I was distraught at the time, as you can imagine."

Burns nodded to show that he could.

"When she came by I was vulnerable," Mrs. Hart said. "I may have blurted out some things I shouldn't have. I don't often let my guard down, but Mary was very comforting."

Burns thought that Mason was many things to many people. Capable of anything.

"I have things under control now," Mrs. Hart said, and Burns wondered if she really did. The rigid posture, the tightly held emotions, the dry tone of her voice seemed to him to be indicative of repression rather than control. But maybe that was the same thing. He wasn't sure. After all, he taught English, not psychology.

"You must have had a lot of visitors," Burns said.

"Oh, yes. Everyone loved Matthew. Quite

a few of his colleagues have been by to see me, and I appreciate it."

She smiled a very small smile to let Burns know that he, too, was appreciated.

Burns asked if any of the college's board members had been by to see her.

"Of course. They realize what a valuable contribution Matthew made to the college, and they wanted to let me know that."

"The Balls must have come by," Burns said. "Neal Bruce. Robert Yowell. Steven Stilwell."

"The Balls were very thoughtful. They brought a nice casserole."

Burns wondered where they'd bought it, but he didn't say so. He was sure Karen Ball hadn't actually cooked it herself.

"Neal was our banker for years," Mrs. Hart said. "He doesn't do much now, of course, but he came by. The others didn't, but they might not have known Matthew well."

"He'll always be remembered at the college," Burns said, and after a few more minutes of superficial talk, he managed to leave more or less gracefully. He felt sorry for Mrs. Hart, and there was nothing he could do to make her loss any less painful. But maybe he could help catch her husband's killer.

Burns's next stop was Dean Partridge's house. When Burns arrived, Billy was nowhere in sight. That didn't mean anything, however, as Burns well knew that the goat was quite depraved and capable of waiting in concealment for anyone who was so foolish as to let his guard down.

Burns looked around warily before he got out of the car to be sure that Billy wasn't lurking behind a bush or hiding behind the corner of the house. There was no sign of him, and no movement, so Burns figured the coast was clear. He got out of the car and went up to the front door.

"Been mowing the lawn?" Dr. Partridge said when she came to the door and got a look at Burns's outfit.

"Practicing for the big game," Burns said.

"I'm sure the students are shaking in their boots," Partridge said, leading him into the den. "Sit down and tell me what's so urgent that you have to meet me at home."

Burns sat on the couch and looked around at the cabinet where the toy soldiers should have been, the toy soldiers that were the cause of all the trouble.

"You said something when we were talking about the people that came through this room," Burns told her. "I've been wondering about it today."

"I said quite a few things. Would you like something to drink before we go over them again?"

Burns said he didn't think so, and Dr. Partridge asked what specific thing she'd said that Burns was wondering about.

"You told me that Steven Stilwell was above suspicion. You said he was an honest man and that you were sure of it, but you didn't tell me why. I'd like to know."

"Why?"

"I think Mary Mason lied to us about him. I don't think she actually saw him alone in the room."

"I told you that she was capable of anything."

"And I believe it," Burns agreed, without going into his reasons. "But that doesn't explain why you think Stilwell is innocent."

"But you just said yourself that Mary was lying about him. Why would she do that, by the way?"

"That's confidential information," Burns said. He'd tell Napier, but he didn't see that Dr. Partridge needed to know. "And the fact that she was lying doesn't have anything to do with why I'm asking about him. So what's the deal?"

"I'm sure most of the faculty members are

aware that I'm a very sentimental person."

It was all Burns could do not to laugh. Most of the faculty considered Dean Partridge a real hardcase.

"So you're sentimental about Stilwell?" he said.

"That's right. The man is a treasure, always giving his time to the college, always helping out when he can. And do you know why?"

Burns had his suspicions, but he said that he had no idea.

"Because he's had a tragic life. He's really very lonely. It's a sad story, and I feel sorry for the man."

Burns thought that he might have guessed part of the story. Stilwell had been married at one time, but Burns had noticed that there were no photos of his family in his office.

"I know his son didn't do well here at the college," Burns said.

"He had a bad semester. Steven told me all about it."

Burns knew about the bad semester. He'd checked the grades that evening in his office. Hart's class hadn't been the only one that young Taylor Stilwell had failed that semester. He'd also failed Mal Tomlin's class, Don Elliott's class, and Abner Swan's class. An interesting series of names, and those had been the only classes he was taking.

"Tell me what happened," Burns said.

"I don't see why this is important. Steven has had some bad things happen in his life, and he couldn't possibly have killed anyone."

"I'm not so sure about that."

"Well, you should be. To accuse him of such a thing is simply outrageous."

"No, it's not. Everyone's a suspect. You know that."

Partridge had to think about that for a while. Burns waited patiently until she'd made up her mind.

"You're right, of course," she said. "I shouldn't let sentiment interfere with logical thought. But I'd like to know why you suspect him."

"Because he knew something he shouldn't have known," Burns said, and let it go at that.

"I'd like for you to be more specific."

Burns sighed. "Mary Mason knew that there was a soldier found by Matthew Hart's body. She knew because Mrs. Hart told her. But Mrs. Hart says she didn't tell anyone else, and it wasn't in the papers. Mrs. Hart couldn't have told Stilwell, because he didn't go by to offer his sympathies."

"That's very thin evidence."

"I know. But Neal Bruce and the Balls went by to see Mrs. Hart, and they didn't know about the soldiers. Stilwell did. I think he knew because he put it there."

"But he would have to have a reason. What R.M. would call a motive."

Burns thought about those four failing grades. And the fact that he could find no other records of Taylor Stilwell's having enrolled at HGC. He knew that wasn't reason enough for murder, but maybe there was more to the story.

"I thought maybe you could help me with that," he said.

"Not really," Partridge said. "What happened to Steven is a sad story, but that's all it is."

"I'd like to hear it anyway," Burns said, and so Partridge told him.

Chapter 32

According to Dr. Partridge, Steven Stilwell, dealer in antiques and strong supporter of Hartley Gorman College, was a product of the 1960s, which of course didn't end until well into the 1970s. Born in 1953, he had entered college during the Vietnam era and found a home in the anti-war movement, a movement with which Dr. Partridge had a great deal of sympathy, having been involved herself.

"So you can see that Steven would never kill anyone," she said. "He was a pacifist."

Burns remembered his earlier theory that Hart's killer might only have been trying to scare him. Tomlin and Elliott hadn't been killed, though in Elliott's case it had been a near thing.

"Sometimes pacifists do funny things," Burns said, without being more specific about past events at HGC. He was sure Partridge would remember without his saying anything further. She had been involved in those events as much as he had. More, really. Murder had been only a part of the resulting mess, and things hadn't turned out well for all concerned in spite of Burns's helping Napier pin things down again.

"Anyone might go wrong, I suppose," she said. "But not Steven. His son was killed, you know."

Burns hadn't known, and he told her so.

"Steven doesn't talk about it much. I think he talked to me only because my own past had certain elements in common with his. He told me that when it happened, he couldn't believe it. He went deeply into denial. It took years for it to sink in. He wasn't so closely involved with the college at the time. That came later, and I think he works so much with us now because his business doesn't keep him fully occupied. He needs other activities to keep his mind off his troubles. His wife left him after their son was killed, and that didn't help matters, I'm sure."

"Did his wife blame him for Taylor's death?"

"I believe so. Steven and his son were very close. Taylor was named for Steven's best friend, who had moved to Italy to become some sort of antiques broker. In fact, he was in business there for a while, but then there was a huge scandal, something to do with the graffiti at Pompeii. Whatever he did, it was a serious offense, and he was tossed into an Italian prison. That was long ago, and I don't believe he's been released yet."

Burns was tempted to tell her, as he sometimes did his freshman writing students, that what she had said was interesting but off the subject. It had nothing to do with the topic under discussion. But he didn't think Dr. Partridge wanted any lessons in organization at the moment.

As if she knew what he was thinking, she said, "I know that's not what you wanted to hear, but I wanted you to know at least one of the reasons Steven and his son were so close. The son took the place of the person who was gone, and they were great friends. But Steven set very high standards for his son, and he was quite disappointed when he didn't make the grade here at HGC."

Burns wasn't sure where all this was going. He didn't see what it had to do with the son's death or with Stilwell's wife's leaving him.

"You haven't told me how the son died," he said. "That might be relevant."

"Oh, it is. But not in the way you think. It just proves that Steven couldn't possibly be a killer."

"I'd still like to hear about it."

"Very well. Steven's son was killed in the first Gulf War."

Burns mulled that over. "I didn't think there were many American casualties in that one."

"There weren't. But if your son is one of them, the small number doesn't mean a thing."

That was easy to agree with. And while Burns didn't yet see what the death of Taylor Stilwell had to do with anything, it did provide the missing military connection. So maybe there was more to the story than he'd yet heard.

"I don't see how Stilwell's wife could blame him for their son's death anyway," Burns said.

"She blamed him because of the pressure he put on Taylor to do well."

"How could that have caused his death?"

"It was his grades," Partridge said. "When Taylor failed all his classes, Steven was very upset. He told Taylor that he couldn't continue to pay for his education if Taylor was going to waste it. He told him that he would either have to redeem himself by going back to school and making all A's or getting a job."

"Making all A's is tough," Burns admitted. "And parents can be very demanding."

He remembered that over the years he'd had a number of students in his classes who'd become increasingly nervous about their grades as the semester went on because they were so afraid of disappointing the parents who were paying for their educations. He'd had enough of them in tears in his office to know how heartbreaking the pressure, whether real or imagined, could be.

"Let me make a guess," he said.

"Could I stop you?"

"You're the dean. You could tell me to get out of here and go home."

"But I'm not going to do that. Make your guess."

"All right. Here it is: Taylor Stilwell didn't get a job after he flunked out. He joined the Army."

Burns could see the twisted logic of it. The son would spite the father by doing exactly the thing that would hurt the father most.

"That's right," Partridge said. "And he got sent to the Persian Gulf not long after he went through training. He never came home, and his mother blamed Steven. He didn't even argue with her. After all, he blamed himself. So you can see that he couldn't possibly have killed anyone."

Burns didn't see it that way at all. What he saw was a man who had blamed himself for his son's death for years and probably had become embittered by the guilt that, if it had lessened at all over the years, had been brought back in its full force by the new war in the Persian Gulf region. Hearing and reading the stories of the soldiers who had died during the conflict, and who were still dying in the peace, must have aroused powerful memories. If Stilwell had thought about it enough, and tried hard enough to come up with a new rationalization, he might have decided not only that he wasn't to blame for what had happened but that others were. Taylor's instructors, for example. And then he might have decided that they had to be punished.

"Who knows what evil lurks in the hearts of men," Burns said.

Partridge gave him a puzzled look. She clearly didn't know about *The Shadow*. "I beg your pardon?" she said.

"Just something I heard recently," Burns told her.

He wondered now if Stilwell hadn't been taunting him. Knowing that he was a suspect, he had been letting Burns know the truth in a roundabout way.

And then Burns thought about the "accident" of that afternoon. Mary Mason had been parked near Stilwell's store. Had she gone by to apologize about having misled Burns and Partridge about Stilwell's interest in the soldiers?

Burns had thought that her lie had removed Stilwell from suspicion, but Stilwell would have seen things differently. Mason's apology would have reminded him of his conversation with Burns, and he might even have realized that he'd slipped up by mentioning the soldier by Hart's body.

Those soldiers were the clincher for Burns. He was convinced that Stilwell had indeed taken them and that he'd planned all along to use them in his revenge scheme. It would be another example of his cleverness, leaving behind a clue that pointed to something buried in the past, something he didn't think anyone would connect with him.

Mason had known where Burns was going that afternoon. He hadn't thought about her because he would have recognized her Cadillac under any circumstances. He had no idea what kind of car Stilwell drove, but now he figured it was Stilwell who had showed up on Thrill Hill.

Maybe Stilwell hadn't planned to run him off the road. He might have been on his way to some vantage point where he could shoot Burns with the .22 when he came out of the Codys' mansion. But Burns had left too soon, so Stilwell had taken a chance, the only chance he had, to get rid of Burns by forcing him off the road. Burns was glad it hadn't worked out.

"It was Stilwell all along," he said.

Partridge said that she didn't believe it. "And I won't condone your going to the police with that idea."

"I'm sorry you won't," Burns said, "because I'm going to do it anyway. I was hoping you'd see it the way I do."

"I can't. I just can't believe that Steven would do those things."

"I'm not asking you to believe it, but I'd like for you to accept the possibility. I'll just tell Boss Napier what I suspect. He's the one who has to make the final determination about an arrest, anyway. I'll give him the information and let him decide. You can talk to him, too, and tell him your side of the story. If his investigation doesn't turn anything up, then Stilwell isn't harmed, and in fact, he'll be relieved to know that he's no longer under any suspicion."

"I couldn't stop you in any case," Partridge said.

"That's right. If you don't mind, I'll use

318

your phone to call Boss Napier."

"I mind," Partridge said, "but I won't try to stop you. There's a phone in the kitchen if you want privacy."

She pointed the way, and Burns went to make the call.

Chapter 33

Boss Napier didn't really believe it, either.

"Sure, the guy's a little sleazy." He paused. "Don't tell Gwen I said that, all right?"

"I promise," Burns said, but he had his fingers crossed.

He was sitting at Dr. Partridge's kitchen table, but Partridge was nowhere around. She hadn't wanted to tell Napier her side of the story.

"Anyway," Napier went on, "Stilwell's a little sleazy, but he doesn't come across like a killer."

Burns mentioned his theory that Stilwell hadn't meant to kill anyone.

"Maybe he's just not a very good shot," Burns said.

"Could be. If that's so, then Don Elliott is one lucky guy."

"He's not dead, so I'd say he was lucky whether Stilwell's a good shot or not."

"We don't know it was Stilwell. So don't talk like he's already convicted."

"I'm sure he's the guilty party. The rest is

up to you. You'll have to get the proof. Find the rifle, find out that he was in the vicinity when Don was shot, find the rest of the soldiers. Whatever."

"Are you trying to tell me how to do my job?"

"Not me," Burns said. "I'm just an English teacher, and from now on, I'm going to stick to teaching students the difference between iambic pentameter and anapestic hexameter."

"Are you talking dirty, Burns?"

"Never mind. I think Stilwell's guilty. You can either prove that he is or that he's not."

"What does Gwen think?"

It still wasn't easy for Burns to think of Dean Partridge as *Gwen*. He said, "She thinks I'm crazy. She insists that Stilwell didn't to it."

"I was afraid of that. She's not going to like it if I prove that he's guilty."

"Maybe he's not. It's your job to find out, one way or the other. She can't blame you for doing your job."

"You don't know much about women, do you, Burns?"

Burns had to admit that Napier was right.

"Well, I do. And I know that Gwen will be mad at me if I put Stilwell in jail. It won't matter if he was responsible for everything from the disappearance of Jimmy Hoffa to the collapse of Enron."

Burns had to smile at the idea of Boss Napier as an expert on women. But then who was he to judge?

"You can't let what she thinks keep you from doing what you're paid and sworn to do."

"I know that better than you do, Burns. I'm just telling you what's going to happen, and it's all your fault."

Burns wanted to bang the phone on the table, but he restrained himself.

"It's not my fault," he said. "I didn't even want to be involved, but you and Dr. Partridge insisted. It's not my fault that things didn't turn out the way you thought they would."

"Whatever you say, Burns."

"Don't put it that way. Are you going to arrest Stilwell or not?"

"I can't arrest him on what you've given me. I'll have to get a warrant and find that rifle. Or those soldiers. Isn't that what you told me I needed to do?"

"I give up. You're hopeless."

Burns started to hang up, but then he thought of something.

"You'd better have someone watching

Abner Swan," he said. "He was the other instructor that Taylor Stilwell had when he flunked all his classes."

"And you think Stilwell might make a try for him?"

"That's right. Why wouldn't he? It fits the pattern of what's happened so far."

"The pattern you've worked out. But maybe that's not the shooter's pattern."

"Right. Whatever you say."

This time Burns did hang up. He looked around for a telephone book, but he didn't see one, and he didn't want to rummage through Dr. Partridge's kitchen. He went back in the den and asked where the phone book was. Dr. Partridge went into the kitchen with him and got it out of a cabinet drawer.

"I need to make another call," he told her, and she left the room again.

Burns looked up Abner Swan's number. Swan's wife, who was usually unbearably chipper, answered on the first ring and told him that Abner would speak to him in "just a jiffy." She put the phone down on a hard surface and called her husband. In a couple of seconds, he came on the line.

"Abner," Burns said, "I think you might be in danger. I think you should stay inside tonight. And don't stand in front of any lighted windows."

"Are you trying to scare me, Carl?" Swan said. There was a little quaver in his voice. "Because if you are, it's working."

"It's just that I have a feeling you could be on the list of people the sniper is after. With all that's been happening around here the last few days, you don't want to take any chances."

"You're right about that, my friend, but why me?"

"It's too long a story, and I might be wrong. Just do me a favor, all right?"

"You can count on me," Swan said. "What about tomorrow?"

"I think everything will be settled by then," Burns told him, hoping that he was right.

"I'll stick to the house then. Thanks for the warning."

"You're welcome," Burns said.

Partridge was waiting for Burns in the den after he finished the call, but she didn't ask how his conversation with Napier had gone or who he'd called after talking to the police chief. Instead she thanked him for his help.

"I don't believe you've come to the right conclusion," she said, "but I know you've done your best."

"For what it's worth, Boss Napier agrees with you."

"And he's right. You'll see."

"I probably will," Burns said, and then he left.

When Burns got home, he sat in his car for a few minutes. His house was around thirty years old, and the original owner had never installed a garage door opener. When he bought the house, Burns had thought about getting one, but at the time he hadn't had the money, and later he just hadn't bothered. He didn't mind getting out of the car to open and close the door.

He had long ago lost the garage door key, but that had never proved to be a problem. As far as Burns knew, there had never been any burglaries in his neighborhood, and most people would just assume that a closed door was locked, or, if not locked, held firmly in place by an opener.

But something that Boss Napier said had changed Burns's thinking about getting out of the car.

Getting out and opening the door was a routine for Burns, something he did every time he arrived home. It was dark now, but over the garage door there was a light controlled by a timer. It came on every evening at eight o'clock and went off at ten. So if Burns got out of the car, he'd be well lighted for anyone who might want to take a shot at him.

There were plenty of places for a shooter to hide, too, as Burns lived on the southeast edge of town. Across the street was undeveloped property covered with scrub oak trees and mesquite. There was a carwash down at the end of the block, but it was usually deserted in the evenings. There was only one car there now, parked at the vacuum station where someone was probably cleaning out the interior.

Burns knew he had to get out of his battered Toyota sooner or later. He could, of course, slink down and glide to the front door while trying to keep to the shadows, or he could even go around to the back of the house and get in through the door from the yard.

Or he could just open the garage. After all, Abner Swan was the one in danger, not Burns. If anybody needed to watch his step, it was Abner. Burns had never flunked Taylor Stilwell and in fact had never had him in a class. He had been gone from the college by the time Burns arrived.

Burns looked up and down the street. The houses were quiet. There was no one outside, but then that wasn't unusual. People tended to stay in their homes after dark. They watched TV or read the newspaper. They didn't walk up and down the block to see if there were snipers hiding across the street.

Burns got out of the car and raised the garage door. The little wheels squeaked on the tracks as it rumbled up, and Burns told himself that he would spray some lubricant on them in the morning.

No one took a shot at him, and he felt a little silly for having even thought there was a chance of something like that.

He got back in the car and drove into the garage. Before he got out, he grabbed his baseball glove. The ball he'd hit over the fence the day before was lying on the floor, so he got that, too. Then he got out of the car and pulled down the overhead door.

The door from the garage into the house was located between the washing machine and a stash of Pepsi One in two-liter bottles. Burns bought it on sale and kept it in the garage so he'd always have some available. When he put his key in the door lock, he noticed that one of the bottles was lying on its side. He must have knocked it over when he left for practice, though he didn't remember doing it. He bent down and righted the bottle.

He stood up and turned his door key. There was no resistance, as if the door hadn't been locked. Burns tried to remember if he'd locked it when he left, but he couldn't. He usually did it automatically, but that didn't mean he hadn't forgotten to do it.

He opened the door, went into his kitchen, and flipped on the light.

Steven Stilwell was sitting at the breakfast table. He looked perfectly at home, as if he lived there instead of Burns. The only thing odd about him was that he was holding a pistol. The pistol was pointed straight at Burns.

"The lock on that door is pretty useless," Stilwell said. "I just wiggled the handle really hard a few times, and it opened."

"I didn't know that," Burns said.

"Well, it's true." Stilwell motioned at the kitchen with his free hand.

"I'll get it fixed."

"I don't think you'll be doing that. Did you know this harvest gold crap is really out of style?"

"It came with the house," Burns told him, looking at the pistol rather than at his refrigerator, his stove, his sink, or his cabinet tops.

"You should have bought new stuff."

"I couldn't afford it. And the old stuff worked, so I figured, why bother?"

"Well, it's sort of like the deal with the door lock. It won't matter to you much longer whether it works or not."

Burns didn't like the sound of that.

"Why?" he said.

"Because," Stilwell said, "I'm going to kill you."

Chapter 34

Burns wasn't an especially heroic sort, and he knew that Stilwell meant what he said. But for some reason, Burns wasn't worried.

Maybe it was because it was hard for him to believe that Stilwell would actually pull the trigger of the pistol. Stilwell was, after all, a supposedly mild-mannered guy who sold antiques. Burns had been to his store and talked to him about old radio shows. Could the man who had given Burns a tape of a *Shadow* episode shoot him in cold blood? Burns didn't think so.

On the other hand, Stilwell had already killed Matthew Hart, taken a shot at Mal Tomlin, and wounded Don Elliott. Burns found that he was worried, after all.

"It wouldn't do you any good to kill me," Burns said. "I've already told Boss Napier that you were the one who shot Hart and Elliott."

"As soon as I realized I'd mentioned that toy soldier by Hart's body, I knew you'd figure it out sooner or later. I should never have taken the soldiers, but I liked the idea of leaving them by the bodies. They'd be a sort of symbol."

Being an English teacher, Burns could appreciate symbolism. "Cute," he said.

Stilwell nodded. "Too cute. I should have known that. When Mary Mason came by this afternoon and told me she was sorry she'd sicced you on me, the conversation you and I had about the soldiers came back to me. It was too late for me to do anything about what I said, of course, but I thought I might be able to get to you before you put things together. Mary mentioned that you were going to see the Codys, so I thought I'd get you while you were there. But you got lucky and left a little too soon for me. So I tried to cause an accident. That didn't work either. I should've stopped my car after you went off the road and shot you then."

"Yeah," Burns said. He was sweating a little, though his house was cool. He could hear the air-conditioner running. "But you didn't. Now it's too late."

Stilwell looked calm and relaxed sitting there in Burns's chair. A little scruffy, true, but then he always looked a little scruffy. He smiled.

"It's never too late for some things," he said. "Not for revenge."

"That's what all this is about, isn't it? You

blamed yourself all those years for your son's death, and now you're blaming someone else, and you think they deserve punishment."

"It was their fault Taylor flunked out. The kid screwed up. He knew it, and he asked for a chance. They wouldn't give it to him."

"None of them? Not even Abner Swan?"

Abner Swan was a notorious softie. He'd never heard a hard-luck story he didn't fall for.

"Taylor never got to Swan. He went to Hart to ask if he could retake a test, maybe improve his grade. Hart laughed at him."

Burns wasn't surprised to hear it. And in fact, he wouldn't have blamed anyone who didn't allow make-up work or "extra-credit assignments," as some called them. Students were supposed to do the work when it was assigned, not later. They were supposed to pass the test when it was given, not take it later. To give one student special treatment was to cheat the others.

On the other hand, laughing at students who requested such help was just wrong. Burns had never done it, and he was sure Elliott, Tomlin, and Swan wouldn't have, either. They would all have offered some kind of suggestion that would have allowed

Taylor to salvage his semester. Or at the very least, one of them would have. Swan for sure, but probably Mal and Elliott as well.

"He should have talked to his other instructors before he gave up," Burns said.

"Why? So they could have a good laugh? Bunch of assholes."

"They might have been able to help."

"Well, they didn't. So Taylor enlisted in the Army, and he died. It was their fault."

Burns could have said something about fathers who put too much pressure on their kids. Or he could have said that people have to take responsibility for their own actions. But he knew it wouldn't do any good. Stilwell would never have listened, or if he'd listened, he wouldn't have heard.

"You've been a friend to the college for a long time. What happened?"

"I finally realized that those teachers killed my son. He died like all those other young kids you hear about in the news every day now, and it was their fault."

Burns could tell that Stilwell wasn't going to be reasonable. He'd passed beyond reason several days ago, if not longer.

So Burns just changed the subject. He said, "I think harvest gold is a nice color."

"Maybe it was, thirty years ago," Stilwell

said. "Not now. And don't think you can change my mind about what I'm about to do. I'm already going to prison for killing Matthew Hart, so killing you won't change much."

Burns tried to give Stilwell an out. "I wondered if you meant to kill him. I thought maybe you just wanted to scare him."

"No. I wanted to kill him, and the others, too. I'm just not a very good shot, and I was farther away from them. A .22 isn't all that good for distance shooting, anyway. I probably would just have wounded Tomlin and Elliott if I'd hit them where I intended. But that would have been good enough."

"How about me?"

Stilwell moved the pistol barrel. Not much. Not more than an inch. It was still pointed at Burns.

"You might have noticed that this isn't a .22," he said.

"It looks big. And old."

"That's right. It's one of my antiques, a Colt's Bisley model, the 1894. Named after a place in England where shooting competitions were held. It's old, but it works just fine, and it'll make a pretty big hole in you. Even at a distance."

Burns was getting more and more worried. Stilwell was still calm, still talking in a casual, conversational tone as if they were two pals talking over old times or a movie they'd seen, but this wasn't a friendly chat. Stilwell really was planning to shoot him.

"I liked those two episodes of *The Shadow*. I'd like to hear some more."

"That's not very likely, is it?" Stilwell said. "Not very likely at all."

Burns looked down at his T-shirt and shorts. He was wearing his softball glove on his left hand. "If I'm going to die, I'd like to be a little better dressed."

"Been playing baseball?"

"Not baseball," Burns said. "Softball. See?"

As he said the last word, Burns turned his gloved hand around and showed Stilwell the ball that he held in his glove.

"You any good?" Stilwell asked.

"Not very. How about you?"

As he asked the question, Burns flipped the softball to Stilwell.

There are several things a man who's holding a pistol can do when a softball is tossed to him unexpectedly. He can pull the trigger, he can get out of the way, or he can try to catch the ball.

Stilwell clearly hadn't expected anyone to lob a softball in his direction. He pushed back in the chair and juggled the pistol as if thinking he could catch the ball and keep control of the gun.

Burns didn't wait to see what happened. He flipped the light switch and in the sudden darkness dived to his right, in the direction of the den.

Burns had seen movies in which guys dived to the floor, rolled smoothly into a somersault, and came effortlessly to their feet, ready to run or fight or do whatever else the situation might call for.

Those guys were probably professional stunt men who had more practice at diving to the floor than Burns did. He landed hard on his right shoulder and didn't even try a somersault. He just kept on rolling.

There was no wall separating the den from the kitchen and breakfast area in Burns's house, so he rolled right off the tile floor of the breakfast area onto the carpet of the den.

Stilwell fired the pistol at that point, and Burns heard glass shatter. The muzzle flash briefly lit up the room, but Burns didn't pause to assess the damage. He just kept rolling.

There was another shot, followed by quite an explosion, and Burns was showered with glass from his TV's picture tube. He ignored the glass, made a turn to the right, and rolled into the short hallway leading to his front door.

As soon as he felt the cool hallway tile under him, he got up and ran to the front door. He stuck out his arm so he wouldn't hit the door, and when he touched it, he dropped his hand to the knob, turned the lock, opened the door, and ran outside.

His ears were ringing from the gunshots, but he could hear the garage door going up. He ducked behind a pittisporum bush, but Stilwell was no longer interested in shooting him. When Burns peeked from behind the bush, he saw Stilwell running down the street, heading for the carwash.

The car that Burns had seen parked at the vacuum station was still there. Nobody noticed if a vehicle happened to be parked at a carwash, and that was where Stilwell had left his getaway car.

Burns didn't want him to get away. He ran into the garage, grabbed his cell phone from the Camry, and hustled down the street after Stilwell.

Burns had seen his students manipulate their cell phones as they walked the hallways of HGC, and he was always amazed at their manual dexterity. They could hold the phones in the fingers of one hand while punching in numbers with the thumb of the same hand. Burns couldn't do that even while he was standing still, much less while he was running down the street, so he stuck the phone in the pocket of his shorts and kept on trucking.

Burns hoped that someone else had heard the shots and called the police, but he doubted that anyone had. His own house had been closed, and so were all the others. The shots had sounded like thunder in his kitchen, but they might not have been heard even in the houses next door.

Stilwell reached the carwash and grabbed at the car's door handle.

"Stop!" Burns called, forgetting for a moment that Stilwell was armed and dangerous.

He remembered almost immediately, however, because Stilwell looked up in surprise and saw him. Then he lifted his pistol, steadied it with both hands, and fired.

It was a good thing he was a bad shot. The bullet hummed past Burns's ear like a hornet in heat.

Burns stopped running. Surely someone had heard *that* shot and was even now calling the police.

Stilwell fired again and missed again, but Burns realized that stopping had been a mistake. He started running again, in a serpentine pattern, like Alan Arkin in the original movie version of *The In-Laws*. The good one.

Burns wondered how many bullets a Bisley held. Five? Six? More likely the latter, but Stilwell had fired four already.

As Burns neared the carwash, he kicked a rock with one of his sneakers. The rock was a fairly sizeable one, so Burns stopped, picked it up, and hurled it at Stilwell.

He missed, of course. He really wasn't very good at throwing things, either baseballs or rocks. He was going to be in big trouble at the game, assuming he lived to play in the game, that is.

Stilwell didn't try to catch the rock, which bounced off his car's windshield and onto the ground.

Stilwell didn't even look at it. Instead he took another shot at Burns.

That makes five, Burns thought as the bullet tore a strip of asphalt from the street not far from his right foot.

Stilwell left his car and ducked into one of the carwash bays. Burns stopped right where he was and looked around. Nobody was driving by, but maybe the police were on the way. He pulled his cell phone from his pocket and dialed 911. To do that, not being as dexterous as his students, he had to look at the phone. So he didn't see Stilwell step out of the bay and take aim at him.

He didn't hear the shot, either, but he felt the bullet hit him. It tore into the top of his shoulder, and his arm went numb. He dropped his cell phone and heard it hit the street. He felt blood running down his arm, but it still took a couple of seconds for him to realize that he'd been shot.

"Son of a bitch," he said.

Stilwell smiled at him and pulled the trigger again.

Chapter 35

The hammer of the Bisley fell on an empty chamber.

"That was six!" Burns yelled, and he charged toward Stilwell.

He didn't feel much like charging. He knew he was losing a lot of blood, because it was dripping off his fingers now, and his right arm was flapping loosely at his side. It still didn't hurt, however. Burns figured that he was in shock, and that the pain would come later. That was fine with him. The later, the better.

Stilwell had ducked back into one of the carwash bays, no doubt to reload. Burns was going to get him before he could do that little job, and he dug his left hand into the pocket of his shorts where he kept his change. Stilwell had a gun, after all, so Burns needed one, too. And he thought he knew where he could get one.

When he reached the carwash, Burns jogged quietly around to the far end of the bays. There were four of them, and he thought Stilwell had ducked into the second one.

Burns went into the first bay and pulled a quarter from his pocket. He checked the little dial on the coin box. It pointed to "Soap," so Burns inserted his quarter and pulled the pistol grip washing gun from its rubber holster. Gripping the gun in his left hand, he walked across the bay, hoping the hose was long enough to reach into the next alcove. He saw that it was when he stopped at the wall. He had several feet left to play with.

Burns took a deep breath and peeked around the wall. Stilwell stood in the bay about ten feet away, facing in the opposite direction. He was jamming a cartridge into his Bisley and obviously had no idea that Burns was anywhere around.

Burns, remembering the Code of the West, said, "Thisaway, Stilwell, if you're looking for me."

Stilwell slapped the Bisley's cylinder into place and turned, raising the pistol to fire.

Burns pulled the trigger on the washing gun, sending a burst of hot, soapy spray into Stilwell's face.

Stilwell pulled the trigger of the Colt, but the bullet went well wide of Burns and thwanged off the brick wall of the bay and sailed on outside. Burns walked toward the antiques dealer, keeping the jet of water directed at his eyes.

Stilwell fired again. Burns didn't know where the bullet went, but he did know that he'd gone as far as he could go. The hose wouldn't reach any further. So he stopped where he was and continued to spray Stilwell, who was beginning to look like a midget sasquatch taking a bubble bath.

Stilwell started to back away, and Burns dropped the spray gun. He grabbed the long handled brush from the wall of the bay and brought it down hard, whacking Stilwell's gun hand. Stilwell dropped his pistol, and when he stooped to pick it up, Burns smacked him on the back of the head.

Using his left arm, Burns couldn't develop much power, but the metal handle made a satisfactory clonking sound when it met Stilwell's skull. Stilwell dropped to his knees, and Burns moved close enough to kick the pistol out of his reach. Then he hit Stilwell again. It felt good. Burns did it again.

Stilwell fell on his face near the drain. Burns stuck the brush back in its holder and went to the coin box. He had another quarter, so he turned the dial to "Soap" and put the money in the slot. He was standing over Stilwell, hosing him down with the soapy water, when Boss Napier and the rest of the Pecan City Police Department arrived.

It was a great day for baseball, Burns thought. The sun was shining, but it wasn't hot, just pleasantly warm. There was a slight breeze, but not enough to affect the flight of the ball should someone get lucky enough to hit the old pill high into the air. There was a good crowd at the game, and while the students had by far the largest and most vociferous fans, the faculty had a fair number of rooters.

Among them was Burns. He recalled having read that in World War II, soldiers sometimes referred to their "million-dollar wound." That was the one that got them sent home, and that was the kind that Burns had.

He hadn't been sent home, but he'd spent a few hours in the emergency room the previous night, and now he was sitting in the stands with a heavily bandaged shoulder as he watched the game. He wasn't seriously hurt, though there was a small chunk of flesh missing that he wished he had back. He didn't like the idea that it had been torn away by Stilwell's bullet. He'd been given some pills for any pain he might feel, but at the moment he felt just fine. And he had good reason.

Stilwell was in jail, and earlier that day, Burns had been treated pretty much as a hero when he walked into the church before Hart's funeral. Elaine had said that she was filled with admiration for Burns's bravery and had hinted that when his shoulder was better there might be some activities they could try out for rehab purposes. Burns was ready to get started.

Dean Partridge, in spite of her regret that Burns had been right about Stilwell, had congratulated him on a job well done and let him know that if anyone ever got a merit raise, Burns would be at the top of the list. Since as far as Burns knew, no one at HGC had ever received a merit raise, he wasn't too excited at the prospect, but it was nice to be thought of as someone who deserved one.

Boss Napier had, of course, excoriated Burns for being an idiot who should have called the police sooner. Burns had tried to explain that he hadn't been in a position to do so, but that hadn't mollified Napier.

"You could've been killed," he'd said. "If your neighbors hadn't called, you'd be lying on the street with a bullet hole in you. Not that I'd care, except that it would make the department look bad."

"But you look good now," Burns had told him. "You've captured a cold-blooded killer and saved the life of the bungling English teacher."

"Yeah," Napier said. "I gotta admit that's gonna look good in the headlines. I was a little surprised that Stilwell was the perp, though."

Who knows what evil lurks in the hearts of men? Burns thought. But he didn't say it out loud. He wasn't sure Napier would care for philosophy at the moment.

Napier certainly wouldn't be interested now. He and Dean Partridge were sitting in the stands, sharing peanuts from a paper bag. Mary Mason was there too, though not with Neal Bruce. She was unescorted, and even the males among the student population couldn't resist a few appreciative glances in her direction. She was sitting beside Dr. Partridge, who Burns thought had better keep an eye on Boss Napier. If she didn't Mason would be sharing the peanuts instead of Partridge.

Burns sat a couple of rows above them, watching Elaine turn the double play at second base. She looked wonderful in her shorts, with her red hair tucked up under her baseball cap and a red pony tail dangling out the back.

When Elaine had volunteered to take his place, Burns had been amazed. But it turned out that she was a much better second baseman than he had been, not that he would ever admit it. He didn't have to, thanks to his wound. Now he could spend the rest of his life telling everyone how well he would have done in the game if only he hadn't been shot in the pursuit of evildoers and thus deprived of his chance at athletic stardom.

If anyone ever asked him to play in another game, he would jump at the chance. And then he would grab at his shoulder and say, "Wow, that smarts. I was shot, you know. But let me get my glove, and I'll see if I can play."

Everyone would admire his courage, and when his arm just wasn't up to the strain, everyone would understand and ask him to tell the story again of how he'd foiled the master criminal at the risk of losing his own life and how he'd won the shoot-out at the carwash.

And if Boss Napier was nowhere around, Burns would tell them.

About the Author

Bill Crider is the author of more than fifty mystery, western, and horror novels. His work has been nominated for both the Anthony and Shamus awards. His novel *Too Late to Die* won the Anthony for Best First Novel, and "Chocolate Moose," a short story written in collaboration with his wife, Judy, won the Anthony for Best Short Story. It appears in the collection *Death Dines at 8:30*. Bill is most famous for his Sheriff Dan Rhodes mysteries.